1-2-3 SCREAM!

Books by R. U. Ginns

1-2-3 Scream!

Mikey Way

Delacorte Press

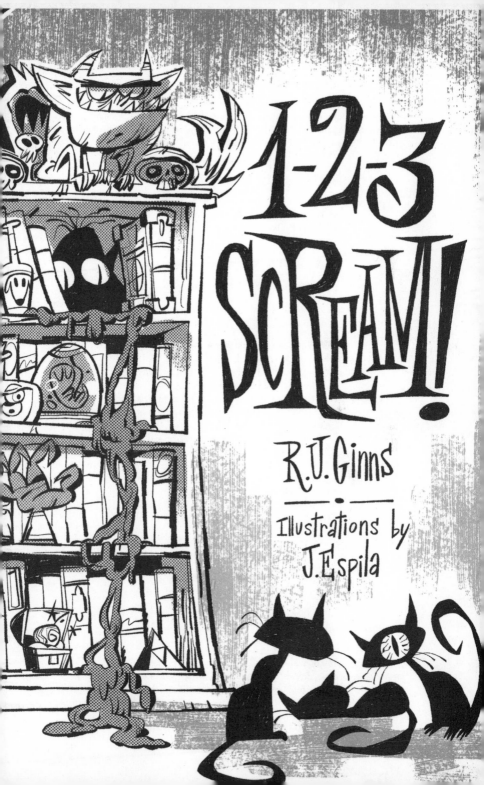

1-2-3 SCReAM!

R.U. Ginns

·

Illustrations by J. Espila

Text copyright © 2022 by Russell Ginns
Cover and interior illustrations copyright © 2022 by Javier Espila

Visit us on the Web! rhcbooks.com

Educators and librarians, for a variety of teaching tools, visit us at RHTeachersLibrarians.com

Library of Congress Cataloging-in-Publication Data
Names: Ginns, R. U., author. | Espila, Javier, illustrator.
Title: 1,2,3, scream! / R.U. Ginns ; illustrated by Javier Espila.
Other titles: One, two, three, scream!
Description: First edition. | New York : Delacorte Press, [2022]
Audience: Ages 8–12. | Summary: Ten humorously terrifying tales that include a villainous vending machine that eats kids like candy, a birthday-party crashing robot, an evil app that can predict exactly how anyone who uses it will die, and more.
Identifiers: LCCN 2021050644 (print) | LCCN 2021050645 (ebook)
ISBN 978-0-593-37407-8 (hardcover) | ISBN 978-0-593-37411-5 (ebook)
Subjects: CYAC: Horror stories. | Humorous stories.
LCGFT: Horror fiction. | Humorous fiction.
Classification: LCC PZ7.1.G575 Aad 2022 (print)
LCC PZ7.1.G575 (ebook) | DDC [Fic]—dc23

The text of this book is set in Goudy Oldstyle Std.
Interior design by Jen Valero

Printed in the United States of America
10 9 8 7 6 5 4 3 2 1
First Edition

Random House Children's Books supports the First Amendment and celebrates the right to read.

This book is dedicated to anyone reckless enough to read it.

—R.U. Ginns

For my wonderful daughter, Marina, who has supervised every single one of the illustrations in this book. And for the doctors Laura, Marta, Silvia, Guiomar, and Miguel Ángel of the pediatric oncology team at the Hospital Materno-Infantil, Malaga (Spain), who saved her life and the lives of our entire family.

—J. Espila

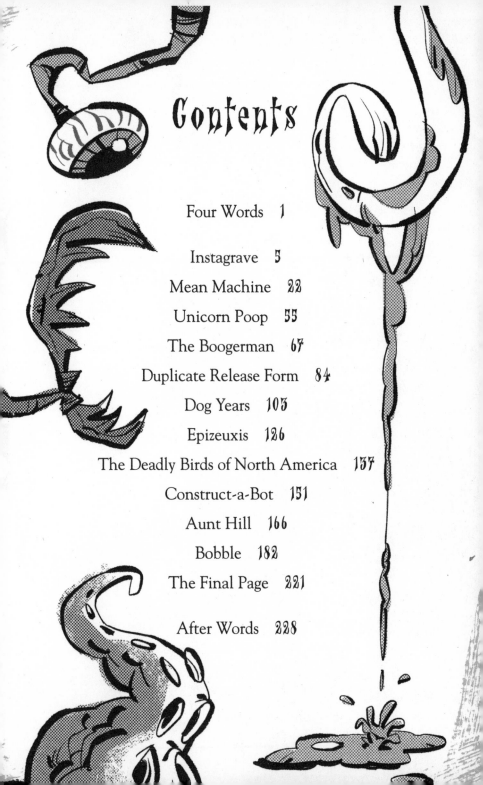

Contents

Four Words

Everywhere I go, readers ask me, "R. U. Ginns?"

I have to admit it's a very good question.

Almost always, my answer is "Yes."

I *am* R. U. Ginns, the author of these stories. I am the person who, day after day, night after night, tapped with one finger at my keyboard to create the words you are now reading.

I usually use my index finger. I raise it high above my head and bring it down, with three or four quick taps in a row. Then I stop and I look around. It's important to know if anyone, or anything, is watching. People. Librarians. Birds.

When I am writing in a coffee shop, or in a bus station, or on the floor in the potato chip aisle at a grocery store, my tap-tap-tapping is enough to scare away most people.

Sometimes, when I'm writing in a library, librarians come over and ask me to type "a little quieter, please."

I don't like it when people tell me which words I should type.

A, *little, quieter,* and *please* are four perfectly good words. But I shouldn't have to stop writing *my* words and switch to typing something else just because someone asked me to, even if one of those words is *please.*

I must keep writing my stories.

I cannot stop.

So instead of answering them, I give those librarians my *super-evil glare.* I frown; then I slowly raise one eyebrow and look into their eyes for a long time without blinking. This is the best way to let everyone know that I must keep writing.

When librarians see a *super-evil glare,* they usually stop asking authors to type "a little quieter, please." They almost never ask me what I am writing. And they *never, ever* ask me to consider leaving because it is midnight and the library closed many hours ago.

I only wish my super-evil glare worked on birds. But no, it doesn't. Nothing is powerful enough to scare away crows, or finches, or pelicans. That is why you should *think twice before you go outside!*

So yes. I am the person who typed every letter of every word of every sentence in this book. I tapped and tapped, and when my fingers began to hurt too much, I finished the last story by typing with my *elbows*. Do you know how hard it is to type a whole story with just elbows? Can you imagine how many times I had to go back and fix all the mistakes?

When you type with elbows, it can take a half hour to type just *four words*.

Now.

I.

Am.

Tired.

No four words have ever been more true.

I have typed and tapped and elbowed one hundred thousand, nine hundred and forty-six letters, and I am exhausted.

I am so very tired. And yet, I am not able to sleep.

How could anyone sleep after writing these stories? How could any-one sleep after learning what I have learned?

Every now and then, when I'm not writing, I have to leave my heavily reinforced and booby-trapped living space for some reason—like to go shopping. I drink a lot of lemon tea and I'm a big fan of saltwater taffy, so my supplies run out often. It was during these expeditions when I learned about all the people and events in this terrible collection. And there is no doubt in my mind:

EVERYTHING IN THIS BOOK IS TRUE.

One hundred percent true. That's why I had to write it all down.

I've changed most of the names in these stories for *your* safety. But don't feel too safe. I know I don't.

Now you are in on the secret.

I hope my book brings you hours of fun and guidance. Guidance that might help you avoid the fates that befall the poor subjects of these tales. I hope you find the stories *hilarifying.* I hope you are able to sleep after reading them. Or not.

And now that you have read my foreword, you are ready to read another four words:

One . . .
Two . . .
Three . . .
Scream!

Instagrave

"Wait. What?" asked Monica Green's friend Isabel. She was staring at her phone with a perplexed look on her face.

She showed her phone to Monica as they stood in line for the school bus. It was open to an app called Instagrave. The picture of Isabel's future tombstone filled the screen.

"Pretty strange. Don't you think, Monica?" she asked. "How could I be found without my bones? Where did they go? What's going to kill me?"

Monica looked at the phone, then at her confused friend.

As soon as Instagrave had first popped up mysteriously on someone's phone, it spread like wildfire. The whole school was obsessed with learning how they were going to die. But the answers didn't always make sense. Monica tried to come up with a few things that might result in the kind of death Instagrave described to Isabel.

"A giant mosquito?" Monica asked. "It could suck out your insides."

"It would have to be pretty big," said Isabel. "Otherwise, I don't think it would have enough suction. Wait. That doesn't answer the bone question."

"How about an accident with a fancy kitchen gadget?" Monica suggested.

"Maybe," said Isabel, nodding. "But I don't do a lot of cooking. Kitchen gadgets aren't really my thing."

Monica didn't want to spend any more time thinking about her friend's death. Her whole class would be on the bus soon, and she wanted to learn about her *own* death before they got to Red Ledge Canyon. She reached into her pocket for her phone.

"Hey! Everyone!" Solomon Roy shouted from three places ahead in the line. "I'm going to smash into the ground! See?"

He held his phone over his head. Monica squinted at it along with everyone else. She saw an obelisk beside a crater. Words were carved into the narrow stone monument.

While a dozen kids gathered to peek at Solomon's memorial, Monica stood back. She unlocked her phone and launched Instagrave.

This is the CRASH site of SOLOMON ROY His emergency parachute FAILED to DEPLOY

"Get back in line, everyone!" Ms. Walker ordered. "I need a head count of all my fourth graders before we get on the bus."

As her teacher walked past, counting heads, Monica stared at her phone. A creepy skull filled the screen. Red lights flashed in its eye sockets and . . .

The app crashed.

The screen flickered bright blue for a moment, then faded to black. After a moment, the home screen reappeared.

Monica groaned softly. Her phone had been giving her trouble all week.

Someone tapped her on the shoulder. She turned to see Kayla Brown behind her with a big smile on her face. She held out her phone for Monica to see. On the screen, a selfie of Kayla wore the same happy expression.

"Get ready," said Kayla. "My face is about to rot. One, two, three, four . . ."

As her friend counted, the

smiling face began to shrivel. Monica watched as the skin puckered. It curdled like a bowl of butterscotch pudding left out in the sun for days, except that it happened really quickly—over the course of a few seconds. Kayla's face crumbled away, leaving nothing but a shiny white skull.

". . . twelve, thirteen, go!" said Kayla.

She pressed the lightning bolt button beneath the skull. Drops of blood trickled from the top of the screen, and a hammer and chisel appeared. The tools blinked and rocked. Instagrave was calculating.

A gray marble tombstone appeared. It had scuba goggles and a snorkel carved into the stone above chiseled words. Kayla wrinkled her nose as she read them out loud:

"Hey, Kayla," someone called from behind them

THIS GRAVE IS IN MEMORY OF
KAYLA J. BROWN
SHE THOUGHT SHE WAS RISING
WHILE SHE SWAM STRAIGHT DOWN

in line. "Isn't your family planning to visit relatives in Trinidad this July?"

Monica watched her friend think about it for a moment. Then Kayla's eyes widened.

"It's true," said Kayla. "And they live in a house close to the beach. I'm going to bring goggles and a snorkel and go swimming every day while I'm there."

Monica quickly did the math.

"You only have four months to live," she told Kayla.

Instagrave was amazing, and kind of mysterious, too. Even though Monica really didn't believe the drowning part, she wasn't sure how the app could know when someone was planning to visit a Caribbean island and go snorkeling.

"I only have four months to live," Kayla repeated cheerfully to a boy standing behind her in line.

"Enough with graves!" barked Ms. Walker. "I need twenty-eight butts in twenty-eight seats so we can visit the state park. Let's go!"

The line began to move. As she followed her classmates onto the bus, Monica launched the app again. The skull with the red eyes appeared and disappeared. She heard slippery, sloshing sounds as pale worms crawled into view. They wriggled about and arranged themselves into twitching gray letters:

Monica had reached the bus door. She grasped the railing with one hand and raised her phone with the other. She smiled for the camera and . . .

Her battery died.

"Keep moving!" Ms. Walker shouted.

Monica sighed. She dropped her hands to her sides, still clutching the phone, then trudged up the steps and headed down the aisle. Everyone else was using Instagrave and sharing their dooms. Why wouldn't it work for her?

Several of Monica's classmates held up their phones so she could read the graves and markers as she passed.

Monica felt severely left out. Her classmates were going to be poisoned, flattened, and torn to pieces from the inside out by tree branches. What was going to be her fate? The only dead thing Monica could tell her friends about was her phone battery.

Monica saw an empty seat up ahead next to Ben Sharpe. She felt her luck changing! Everyone called Ben "Mr. Network." He was obsessed with computer games, and coding, and technology in general. He wore a T-shirt with rows of ones and zeros on it. If anyone could help her, it was Ben.

"Hi, Ben," Monica said as she sat down. "Do you have an extra charger I can use?"

"No problem," he replied. "I've got three batteries with me right now, fully charged."

He unzipped his backpack, reached in, and pulled out a battery the size of a sandwich.

"This baby has eighteen thousand milliamps," he told Monica. "But you've gotta check this out first. Look!"

With his other hand, he held up a tablet. The screen was displaying Instagrave.

FOR SEVENTEEN DAYS
BEN SHARPE
SAT ON A SCANNER
THE RAYS FINALLY KILLED HIM
BUT HIS BUTT SURE WAS TANNER!

"Thank you so much," said Monica as she took the battery from him. "I hope you have fun . . . until you're well done."

"Clever," said Ben.

She found a small cord dangling from the battery and plugged it into her phone. By the time they had reached the parking lot at Red Ledge Canyon State Park, her phone was fully charged.

"Welcome to nature," said Ms. Walker as they filed past her and exited the bus. "This may come as a shock to some of you, but there are amazing things to see that aren't on screens, so it's time to stow your phones until we get back on the bus."

None of the kids were excited to hear this news. Some of them groaned.

"I need my phone to take nature photos," someone wailed.

"How will I know when it's time to go home?" another kid asked.

"I said *stow your phones!*" Ms. Walker shouted.

When their teacher used *that* tone, the kids knew they actually had to listen. Soon all twenty-eight fourth graders had tucked their phones into their pockets, purses, or backpacks.

"Stick to the trails, everyone," Ms. Walker called. "Follow me, and watch your step!"

As her classmates headed out of the clearing and into the woods, Monica walked slowly, letting them get ahead of her. She didn't want to wait any longer. Ms. Walker just didn't understand—this was her big chance.

As soon as she made sure that the others were out of sight, Monica took out her phone.

"Come on, come on," she whispered impatiently while Instagrave loaded. The skull appeared and disappeared. The worms spelled out TAKE PHOTO NOW.

Monica raised the phone, tilted her head slightly, and smiled.

Click.

"Not bad," she said, studying her selfie.

She had snapped a good one on the first try. Her hair glistened in the late-morning sun. The rocky ravines of Red Ledge Canyon surrounded the clearing behind her. They formed an excellent backdrop.

At last, she was going to find out her fate.

As she counted to thirteen, Monica stared at her selfie. In the photo, her eyes began to sink slowly into their sockets, sagging like melting marshmallows. Her skin became reddish-green, then yellowish-pink, then bright white. Her hair fell out and her teeth twitched.

Pop! Pip! Pop!

One by one, the teeth burst into tiny clouds of chalky dust.

It was working!

As soon as the photo of her face had become a tooth-less skull, Monica pressed the lightning bolt.

Blood trickled. A hammer and chisel blinked, and a tombstone appeared.

Monica squinted at the words.

It was hard to see the screen clearly in the direct sunlight. She held the phone at an angle and took a step backward. Then another. Then another.

"Monica!" Isabel called out. "Where are you?"

A hundred yards down the trail, Ms. Walker had stopped everyone for another head count. One of her students was missing. The class had backtracked quickly and fanned out around fields, trails, and the parking lot, looking for their absent friend.

"Over there!" Ben called, pointing toward the edge of a clearing. "I see a phone on the ground."

He raced over to the object, picked it up, and examined it.

"I knew it," he said. "This is Monica's. I let her use my charger on the bus. Eighteen thousand milliamps."

He brushed the phone against his pant leg to wipe away the canyon's red dust. Then he stared at the still-glowing screen. Letters had been cut into a marble slab.

Mean Machine

"The Mean Machine is coming! The Mean Machine is coming!"

When Lucas O'Neal heard some kid yelling the alert, he didn't wait around to find out whether it was for one, two, three, or all four of the bullies. He gave up his spot near the front of the book fair line, pushed through a clump of panicking kids, and ran.

Everybody at Simon D. Kehoe Elementary School was afraid of the Mean Machine. Mikey, Emma, Kim, and Patrick were the worst of the worst, and they worked together like a fine-tuned implement of destruction. They interrupted assemblies, demolished art projects, and squished lunches—and nobody, not even the teachers, could do anything about it. Lately, Mikey Hamper, the biggest, bossiest bully of the Machine, had taken to picking on Lucas.

"Outta my way!" a voice roared in the distance.

Lucas shivered—it was Mikey.

At least twice a week, Mikey stole Lucas's sandwich, tore up his homework, or tossed his backpack out a window. Usually, Lucas was too scared to try to stop him. But today was different. Lucas had a pocketful of money for the book fair. He wasn't going to hand it over without a fight—or at least without a chase!

He raced away from the library. Halfway down the hall, he crouched behind a drinking fountain. As he caught his breath, he felt for the cash in his front pocket. He had exactly enough money for *Super Nuclear Action Robot Force #15*. He really needed to know how S.N.A.R.F. would save the planet from the Orbiting Obliterator.

This far away from the book fair, the hall was quiet. Lucas started wondering if *he* had escaped from his own personal obliterator. Maybe Mikey wasn't looking for him today. Maybe he was planning to terrorize someone else.

"Looooooo-cas!" Mikey's voice boomed from the crowd of kids. "Where are you?"

Nope. Mikey was not planning to terrorize someone else today. Lucas crept out from behind the fountain, stood up, and ran as fast as he could.

His heart pounded as he turned a corner, dashed past four empty classrooms, and skidded to a halt.

He sniffed the air.

Paint. Cleaning supplies. Mildew.

No!

There was only one place in the school with that smell. Lucas was in such a mad panic to get away from Mikey, he had just run straight into . . . *Hall R.*

Nobody went into Hall R if they could help it. That was where dented desks, wobbly chairs, and super-slow tablets went. Phones with dead batteries. Video projectors with broken bulbs. The whole school sent equipment there when it didn't work right and no one could fix it.

Kids used a dozen different names for Hall R. Some called it Horror Hall, or just Holler. Others called it Creep Corridor or Awful Alley.

The classrooms were all dark. None of them had seen a teacher or a student for years.

Lucas turned around.

"Where is he?" Mikey's voice echoed from outside Hall R. "I want my cash!"

The Mean Machine was waiting for him. It was too late to go back.

Lucas continued deeper into Hall R. Maybe he could go all the way to the end and out the emergency exit. If he made it that far,

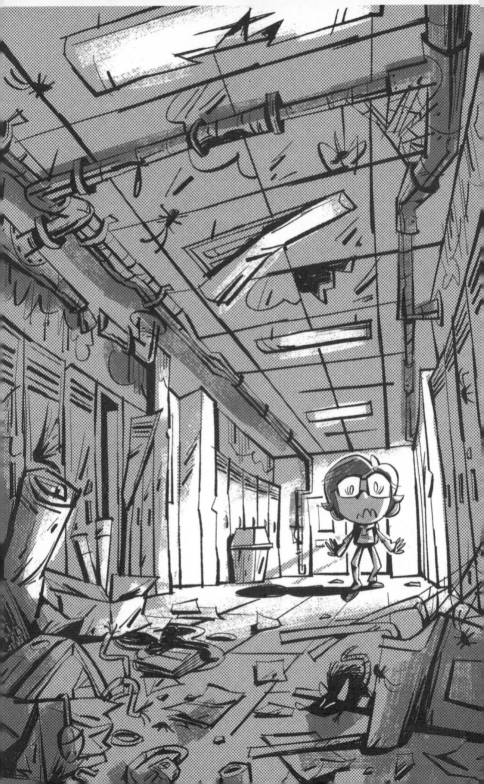

he could cut across the playground to the back of the cafeteria and escape.

He passed rows of lockers long ago rusted shut and rolls of damp, rotting carpets. The air hung thick with dust, and Lucas's nose was assaulted by a dozen gross smells.

He tried really, really hard not to touch anything. Lucas stepped around an abandoned guinea pig cage and kept going. If the guinea pig could escape, maybe he could, too. He hurried past half-crushed cardboard boxes weighed down with broken computer monitors. He passed an empty vending machine and canvas bins in a long line.

He stopped for a moment and studied the machine. It was glowing with a soft neon light, as if it was still plugged in. The inside was stocked with candy of all types, and it looked newer than most of the other equipment in the hall. Lucas thought about putting some money in the machine, but then he remembered he was saving it for the book fair. Besides, who knew how long those candies had been in there?

He peeked into one of the bins next to the vending machine. Spiders skittered to and fro across moldy towels. He shuddered and walked faster.

The hall seemed to go on forever. He thought about calling for a teacher, but there was no point in shouting for help.

No one could hear you scream from Hall R.

Finally, Lucas reached the end of the hall. He looked around for the emergency exit door . . . but it was blocked.

"No, no, no," Lucas moaned.

A stack of broken smartboards leaned against the exit door. Cracks ran across their marker-stained fronts. Frayed cables dangled from their sides. There was nothing smart about them anymore. Lucas gulped as he counted seven big, heavy boards. It would be impossible to move them all. He had no way to reach the emergency exit.

Lucas heard footsteps echoing from behind him. He needed a place to hide . . . now!

Against the wall, he saw a pair of identical gray metal cabinets, about four feet high and three feet across. They rested on crumpled plastic wheels that were never going to roll again. He picked the one on the left, pried open its door, and peeked inside.

Busted computers filled the cabinet: a tangled mess of smashed screens, frayed cables, and chipped keyboards. Lucas dragged out a heavy, dusty printer and set it on the

floor. That made just enough room. He squeezed inside the cabinet and pulled the door shut behind him.

The sound of big sneakers slapping on old floor tiles grew louder and louder. Lucas's heart pounded in his chest as the sound got closer . . . closer . . . .

Suddenly, the footsteps stopped.

Lucas strained his ears, listening hard. Was that Mikey? Was it another member of the Mean Machine? Or even worse, all four?

Lucas tried not to move.

The footsteps started again.

Lucas tried not to breathe.

But wait—now the footsteps were getting quieter, moving farther away from his hiding place. Whoever was out there had given up!

Lucas allowed himself to exhale ever so softly. He might live after all.

Scree-ee-eek!

Lucas heard a high-pitched noise from farther down the hall.

He pressed his ear to the cabinet door.

R-r-r-r-r-runk! R-r-r-r-r-runk!

Thump-a-thump-a-thump-a-thump!

He thought he heard two voices mixed in with all the noises. They

might have been girl voices, but he couldn't tell. And where was Mikey?

Burrrrrrrrrrrrrrp!

What was *that?*

It didn't matter who or what was out there. Lucas was staying hidden.

He pressed against the back of the cabinet and tried to stay perfectly still.

He squeezed his eyes shut, trembling . . . and waited.

Mikey Hamper stopped at the intersection where the four main school hallways met. He shielded his eyes from the flickering fluorescent lights overhead. Somehow, Lucas

had escaped. Not for long, though. The Mean Machine would find him and his book fair money.

Mikey peered into Creep Corridor. The Mean Machine used to hold meetings there. They'd stopped because Kim and Emma said it made their shoes all sticky, so they couldn't sneak up on anyone.

Lucas was too much of a coward to have gone that way. Mikey turned and headed back to the main hall.

Click!

Click!

Kindergarten teachers locked their classroom doors as he passed.

Mikey ignored them, looking for any sign of the twerp. Nothing.

Ahead, the book fair line had re-formed. A dozen chumps waited outside the library, ready to throw away their money. Sure, the book fair sold rubber shark pens and buttons that made loud fart noises, but these kids were probably standing in line to buy books. And a lot of those books didn't even have pictures.

Mikey looked up at a poster on the wall near the library door. He saw a big smiling face and two words along the bottom:

Mikey shook his head. That was ridiculous. He spotted another poster:

That was more like it. He tore the poster from the wall and rolled it into a tube. Then he picked out a small boy standing in line.

Whap-a-whap-a-whap-a-whap!

He swung the poster back and forth, hitting the boy twice on each side of his head.

"Ouch!" shouted the boy. "Why did you do that?"

"I'm *applying* myself," said Mikey. "To your head."

The boy rubbed his ear and looked angry. Mikey raised the poster. The boy quickly turned away from Mikey. He stood on his tiptoes and pretended to see something interesting through the door to the library.

Mikey spotted another target: a girl holding a ten-dollar bill waited for her turn to enter the book fair. He tried to snatch the money from her hand, but she yanked it away just in time.

Mikey grunted. Then he applied himself again.

Whap-a-whap-a-whap-a—

The girl yelped.

Mr. Mink, the science teacher, heard the noise and came out of the science room to investigate. Immediately, the girl rushed over to the teacher and pointed at Mikey.

Last year, when he'd been in fourth grade, Mikey had been in Mr. Mink's science class. It was super boring. They didn't get to do anything with flames or chemicals or even dissect mice. The only reason Mikey passed the class was because Mr. Mink really wanted to get him out of there. For good.

Mr. Mink listened to the girl for a minute as she whined.

Then he waved for Mikey to join them. The teacher hunched his shoulders nervously. His fingers twitched. His eyes darted around like those of a frightened squirrel.

"Um . . . Mikey," said Mr. Mink. "This kind of behavior is . . . uh . . . really . . . uh . . . not acceptable."

Half hidden behind the teacher, the tattletale nodded. Mikey slapped his open hand with the end of the poster. Then he pointed it at Mr. Mink.

"You know what would be *really* not acceptable?" he asked.

The teacher slowly shook his head. He looked good and scared.

"It would be really not acceptable if our principal heard any complaints about any teachers from someone with the last name Hamper," said Mikey.

The teacher gulped.

Hamper was the name on four different car dealerships around town. It was also the name that blinked at the bottom of the twenty-thousand-dollar digital scoreboard Mikey's dad had donated to the school's soccer field. The principal and the school board loved that big electronic sign. It was the main reason that Simon D. Kehoe Elementary School had gotten a blue-ribbon rating last year. There was no way anyone named Hamper was going to get in trouble . . . ever again.

"It would be a *shame* if they had to relocate all the science rooms," said Mikey. "Wouldn't it?"

"Relocate?" the teacher replied nervously.

"Sure," said Mikey. "Wouldn't it be sad if the principal decided to move your class to Hall R? You know . . . where the windows don't open? Where the lights flicker all the time? Way down at the end of Hall R, where all the old, sad, broken things go?"

Of course, Mr. Mink knew of all this and more. Everyone did. The science teacher stood very still. Mikey could tell he was trying to find a way out of this situation. Suddenly, the man's face lit up with a big fake smile.

"What a brilliant science project," said Mr. Mink.

He stepped sideways, putting a few feet between himself and the tattletale. "You're demonstrating the nitrogen cycle."

"He is?" the girl asked, sounding surprised.

"Why, yes," said Mr. Mink. "When Mikey steals book money and uses it to buy snacks, he's . . . um . . . converting paper pages into edible food. Very clever."

Mikey nodded approvingly. Then he glared at the tattletale. Her knees shook.

"Go to the book fair," he barked at her, pointing the rolled-up poster toward the library.

The girl looked relieved. She scurried away to the back of the line.

Mikey would deal with the tattler later. First, he needed to find Lucas. The twerp had gotten away without forking over his money. That story might spread around the school and ruin the Mean Machine's reputation, which would be really not acceptable.

No one escaped from the Mean Machine.

At the end of Creep Corridor, lights flickered.

Maybe Lucas wasn't such a coward after all.

Maybe he was hiding in Hall R.

Mikey tossed the poster on the floor and stomped off to find him.

He passed lockers and dark classrooms. He jiggled the handle of a locker. It wouldn't open. He studied the rust on his hand, then wiped it on his pants leg and kept going.

Mikey kicked an empty, dirty guinea pig cage, and cockroaches scattered.

The air was thick with chemicals.

Cooking grease. Sawdust. Mold.

He wrinkled his nose and kept walking, passing cardboard

boxes and a vending machine. Mikey almost always stopped to check out a vending machine. A lot of the time, you could pound on one with your fists or shake it until it coughed up the goods. But not right now. He had to pound on little Lucas first.

Mikey grabbed a doorknob. It didn't turn. That wasn't a surprise. He had never heard of anyone actually going to classes down here.

Scree-ee-eek!

Mikey looked up.

Was that a scream?

It didn't matter. Even if Lucas yelled for help, it wouldn't come.

No one could hear you scream from Hall R.

"Oh, Loo-cas," he called in a fake, high voice.

Something twitched behind a roll of old carpet leaning against the wall. Mikey walked over and crouched down.

"Oh, little Loooooooooo-cussssss," he said, slowly and more quietly this time.

He pushed away thick tufts of cobwebs and looked behind the smelly carpet. Dozens of gray worms slithered among the fibers. He watched them wriggle for a minute. Then he stood up, flicked a worm, and headed down the hall.

When he reached the exit, it was blocked. Lucas couldn't have escaped this way.

Mikey spotted two gray metal cabinets. Maybe there was something inside worth stealing. He doubted it, but there was no harm in looking. He grabbed the handle of one cabinet and pulled. It creaked loudly as it opened.

The contents spilled onto the floor. He saw crumbling encyclopedias, picture books with cracked covers, and piles of rotted paperbacks. He peered into the cabinet.

Mikey grunted. He didn't see anything valuable. Maybe he'd find something better in the other cabinet. He reached for the handle. . . .

Bam!

Bam!

Mikey turned. Halfway up the hall, by the old vending machine, he saw his friend Patrick dribbling a basketball. Every third bounce, he hurled it against a locker.

Bam!

Patrick Dwyer, the Mean Machine's cocaptain, was a bully, too. And as with Mikey, nobody could do anything about it.

Patrick was only a fourth grader, but he was six and a half feet tall. Because of his height, he played on the high school basketball team. Last November, Patrick had decided to walk around the lunchroom pouring sticky orange soda onto kids' heads. The principal had sent Patrick to detention, and he'd missed basketball practice. The PTA had had the elementary school's water and heat shut off until they let Patrick come back. After that, nobody stopped him from pouring anything on anyone's head again.

Mikey walked over to Patrick and held out his big closed hand.

"Sticks and stones," said Patrick, giving him a fist bump.

"Break some bones," said Mikey.

"Sticks and stones can break some bones" was the official

motto of the Mean Machine. It didn't include the well-known second part about words not hurting anyone.

Mikey leaned to the side and looked past Patrick.

"Are Kim and Emma with you?" he asked.

"No," Patrick answered. "I heard a noise and came down here looking for them."

Bam!

He bounced his ball against a locker again, leaving a big dent.

"They were going to meet me outside the gym five minutes ago," added Patrick. "Strange, right?"

Mikey nodded.

That was unusual.

Everyone knew Kim and Emma Rickles for their punctuality. If they threatened to dunk your head in the toilet at 9:15 a.m., your hair would be dripping wet by 9:16 a.m. If they said they would tie your shoes to the flagpole—with you in them—at 5:00 p.m., you'd be flapping in the air above the school at 5:01 p.m.

The overhead lights flickered, then went out altogether.

For a moment, Mikey and Patrick stood in near darkness, bathed in the soft green glow from inside the nearby vending machine.

Then, just as suddenly, the lights turned on again.

"This place gives me the creeps," said Patrick.

"Don't be a big, tall baby," said Mikey. "It's been raining all day, and really windy. It's probably messing with the electricity."

"I'm not sure about that," said Patrick. "But I do like it when the weather's bad. All the little kids have to stay inside at recess, and there's nowhere to hide. Close-up target practice."

Bam!

"You should take up basketball," Patrick said.

"Nah," said Mikey. "It's not my game."

"Who cares?" said Patrick. "You get to carry a ball around all the time, and nobody can stop you when you accidentally bounce it off somebody's face . . . like this."

Wha-bam!

Patrick whipped his

ball against the front of the vending machine. He threw it so hard the whole machine shook.

"Hey," said Mikey. "You're gonna smash the glass."

"So what?" replied Patrick. "We could take all the stuff inside this thing."

Wha-bam!

He bounced the ball against the machine once more. Then he swiveled and pretended to make a three-point shot.

Mikey leaned forward to see exactly what was in the machine. The glass was scratched and fogged up, but he could see that the things inside . . . looked delicious.

"Kit Kats," he read. "M&M's."

Mikey went back to thinking about Lucas. Actually, he was thinking about the *money* Lucas had brought for the book fair. If he could find the little punk—and his cash—he could buy candy for the whole Mean Machine.

His stomach growled.

Just thinking about it made him hungry. Mikey stood up and held a hand above his eyes to shield them from the fluttering hall lights. He stared down the hallway, looking for any sign of Lucas.

Nothing.

The lights went out again.

Scree-ee-eek!

R-r-r-r-r-runk! R-r-r-r-runk!

A new sound filled the air—a grinding noise, different from the thump of Patrick's basketball. Mikey glanced around to see where it was coming from, but he couldn't make out anything in the blackness.

"What are you doing, Patrick?" said Mikey.

Thump-a-thump-a-thump-a-thump!

More weird noises answered him. Was Patrick running away?

"Don't be such a chicken," Mikey said. "It's just the

Patrick didn't respond.

"They're probably rebooting the scoreboard out on the field," said Mikey. "That usually causes a power surge. I heard the big board uses a ton of power. Like fifty mega-warts, or something."

Burrrrrrrrrrrrrrp!

"Good one," said Mikey.

Out of the corner of his eye, Mikey thought he saw something move. He turned and peeked back, but the only thing there was the green glowing face of the vending machine. He rubbed his thumb against it to wipe away the moisture that had collected on its surface, but it was all inside the glass.

"Help me find that punk, and you can have first dibs on the Sour Patch Kids," Mikey said, squinting at a shiny green-and-yellow package.

Patrick still didn't say anything.

Mikey looked around.

"Patrick?" he asked again.

The hall lights went on.

Patrick was gone. His basketball rolled slowly down the hallway.

Weird. Patrick never left his basketball lying around. But if he wanted to ditch Mikey, then fine.

Mikey watched the ball stop by the blocked exit door.

His stomach growled again.

Enough. He wouldn't waste any more time tracking down Lucas just so he could steal his money and "demonstrate the nitrogen cycle."

Mikey growled—louder than his stomach did.

A big metal box full of candy was within reach. Nobody could stop him.

He studied the vending machine. Below the glass window, a plastic flap covered the long horizontal opening where candy came out . . . and hands went in.

Mikey got down on his knees and reached under the flap. He worked his hand through the wide slot up to his elbow . . . and felt something moist.

"Gross," he said, and tried to pull his hand away.

He couldn't.

His hand was stuck.

He pulled harder.

He felt something wet coiling around his wrist.

Wham!

It tugged on his arm, yanking him into the machine up to his shoulder. His face slammed against the glass.

Through one eye, he saw the candies. They were . . . *moving*. Inside their wrappers, they pulsed and twitched.

Mikey tried to push back against the machine, but everything he touched felt slippery and wet.

Scree-ee-eek!

The slot unhinged like the jaws of a snake and stretched wide apart.

Mikey was yanked through the opening. With one arm caught over his head and his other arm

pinned to his side, he couldn't move. He looked left and right.

R-r-r-r-runk! R-r-r-r-runk!

The panels that lined the sides of the machine rolled up like garage doors. Behind them, the inside walls were pink and lumpy, like the roof of a big mouth.

Long, thin red and white shapes poked out through slits in the rubbery surface. They were hard and pointy, and studded with bumps, like giant crab legs. They began to tap and jab all over Mikey's body.

Suddenly, the crab-leg fingers zipped back into their holes.

The pink walls began to quiver.

Patches of rubbery flesh started to swell in a half dozen places along the sides of the machine. They looked like giant pimples. They grew . . . and grew . . .

They burst open, splattering the inside of the machine with greenish-yellow goo. Sticky fluid dribbled into Mikey's eyes. He clamped them shut, but they still burned.

Something rough and wet slid back and forth across his face. Mikey began to feel pressure all over his head . . . then his shoulders . . . then his back . . . then his chest.

Thump-a-thump-a-thump-a-thump!

Heavy punches battered him from every direction. Wheezing, he drew in as much air as he could.

"Help! Someone! Help!" Mikey screamed. "Kim! Emma! Patrick!"

But he knew as well as anyone: no one can hear you scream from Hall R.

Mikey forced open one eye. Through the slime, he could see the mouth of the machine closing beneath his feet.

"Sticks and stones! Sticks and stones!" he yelled.

No one answered . . . but some bones broke.

The hallway was quiet.

Slowly, Lucas pushed open the door to his hiding place.

He peeked into the hall.

Was it safe?

Cautiously, he stepped out of the cabinet, stretching his cramped limbs.

He didn't see anyone. He didn't hear anyone. Lucas began to walk swiftly back through the corridor, eager to leave Hall R behind. Maybe if it was early enough, he could even get his place back in the book fair line.

His foot kicked something.

A basketball. It looked like the ball Mikey's friend Patrick was always carrying—but what was it doing here?

Curious, he picked it up.

The ball was covered with sticky greenish-yellow goo.

"Yuck," said Lucas, dropping it to the floor.

He watched it bounce and roll. It came to rest next to the old vending machine.

Lucas rubbed his fingertips together. They felt gross.

He started walking again.

Burrrrrrrrrrrrrrp!

A long, deep, watery belch rang out and echoed through the hall. The hair stood up on the back of Lucas's neck. The sound seemed to have come from the vending machine.

Lucas walked back to the machine and peered into it.

The inside was fully stocked, but the glass was fogged up, making it hard to see clearly. Lucas leaned closer and squinted.

In neat rows, candy bars dangled from plastic spiral coils.

Lucas wasn't hungry. He just wanted to go back to the book fair and—

Wait a second.

He looked at the candies again. The labels weren't quite right:

Lucas scratched his head. He bent down and looked more closely at the candy bar on the end of the row. Yellow sludge oozed from one corner of the wrapper.

He stared at the label.

Unicorn Poop

We got home from our vacation to Mammoth Cave National Park at midnight on Sunday. My parents were really tired from driving all the way back from Kentucky, where the park is, so they slept late on Monday. I had to make myself breakfast.

On the way downstairs I stepped on something. It was hard, and bumpy, and rainbow colored.

"Whaaa?" I asked as I bent down to inspect it.

Light from the kitchen window made it sparkle.

I picked it up.

It felt waxy, like a candle.

I sniffed.

It *kind of* smelled like a candle but not quite.

As I studied the red, orange, yellow, and green stripes, my younger sister, Betsy, came up behind me and tapped my shoulder.

"You found unicorn poop," she said.

"This?" I asked, holding out the colorful waxy mound.

"Yes," she answered. "And that means a unicorn has been in our house."

My sister read books about magical animals all the time. If anyone in the family was going to detect signs of a unicorn, it would be her. I examined the lump.

"It might still be here," she

said, looking at something past my shoulder. I turned around.

Betsy pointed at the floor, then bent down and picked up something blue, indigo, and violet.

"Unicorns are magical rainbow-powered creatures," she said, waving the object in front of my face.

"Hold still," I said, and squinted at it.

I noticed some bits of gray and black. I was pretty sure those weren't colors of the rainbow.

Betsy took two long sniffs. Then she nodded at me.

"It's fresh," she said. "Come on."

Together, we went searching for the magical beast.

We thought we saw something moving behind the living room curtains, but it was just a breeze coming from the open window. We searched under the coffee table, and beneath all the living room furniture, too. I found a library book that was five years overdue, but no unicorn.

There weren't any magical creatures in the kitchen either.

Then, while Betsy opened cabinets and took out all the pots and pans, I got down on my hands and knees and checked under the table.

I spotted a trail of turquoise and magenta lumps.

"Help me move the refrigerator away from the wall," I told my sister.

She came over, but before we could shove anything, my dad walked into the kitchen.

"What are you two doing?" he asked.

"We're finding a unicorn," I told him.

"Now's not the time for playing pretend," said my dad. "You're both late for school."

"Unicorns are very special animals," said Betsy as she picked up several colorful chunks and dropped them into her backpack. "They bring tons of good luck."

That sure didn't happen.

On the way to school, it started pouring rain, and Betsy got struck by lightning! Her shoes disintegrated, and she lost both of her eyebrows. Not lucky at all.

I forgot about the unicorn for the rest of the day. Then, on Tuesday, after we came home from visiting Betsy in the hospital, my dad stepped on something blue-green and red-violet at the top of the stairs. He slipped and fell down the stairs. The doctor said he had three cracked ribs and two broken teeth. Very unlucky.

That evening, I saw my mom hunched over her desk staring at a pile of papers and forms and hospital bills. She looked really tired and worried.

"I thought unicorns bring tons of good luck," I said.

"Unicorns?" she asked.

I held out a poop I had just found. It was brown, with rose-colored stripes.

My mom inspected the lump in my hand and picked out a small bit of paper.

"Burnt sienna," she read, and started to chuckle.

I didn't get what was so funny.

She picked out another paper bit.

"Carnation pink," she said, and laughed even harder.

She thought something was hilarious, but I didn't know what. Her laughter went on and on. After a while, it didn't sound funny. Maybe all the bad luck was getting to her.

"Mom?" I asked. "Are you okay?"

She chuckled harder. She couldn't stop. Then she bumped a glass of water with her elbow. Liquid spilled onto her keyboard and across her desk. It flowed over the edge and rained onto a power strip. Sparks flew. Her sleeve caught on fire, and she stopped laughing. All the lights went out in the house.

Our neighbor Mr. Rosenzweig walked over to complain about the noise. He let himself in, but a bookshelf tipped over in the hallway. It landed on his foot and he limped home. Later, he came back to get his big toe. He left again without saying anything.

Nobody in my family talked to me about any of the things that happened. Maybe they blamed me for some of the bad luck. Maybe they were scared. So I was glad when Uncle Hayden arrived. He was never scared to talk about anything to anyone.

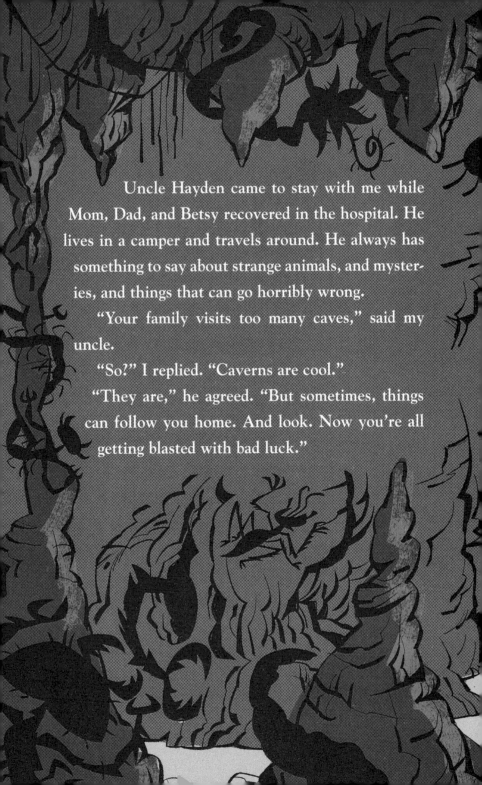

Uncle Hayden came to stay with me while Mom, Dad, and Betsy recovered in the hospital. He lives in a camper and travels around. He always has something to say about strange animals, and mysteries, and things that can go horribly wrong.

"Your family visits too many caves," said my uncle.

"So?" I replied. "Caverns are cool."

"They are," he agreed. "But sometimes, things can follow you home. And look. Now you're all getting blasted with bad luck."

We were having terrible luck, that was for sure.

"It could be a skrank, or a gremlin," he told me. "They're really unlucky. Or maybe there's some type of jinx beast hiding in your house. The dark green ones play mean tricks on people. It's never funny."

"No," I said, showing him one of the rainbow chunks. "It's a unicorn. They're supposed to bring us *good* luck, not bad."

Uncle Hayden squinted at the yellow-green and red-violet lump.

"It looks like Roxy has been eating your art supplies," he said.

I stared at the thing in my hand. He was right. It wasn't unicorn poop. It was crayons pooped out by our *dog*.

"Roxy!" I called as I searched the house. "Where are you?"

In the den, a line of dandelion- and apricot-colored blobs led across the carpet. At the end of the trail, I saw a tail wagging behind the sofa.

"You've been a bad girl, Roxy," I said, rounding the corner, and . . .

A strange creature was kneeling on the floor between the sofa and the wall. It looked like a shriveled little person, dressed in some kind of animal fur. Its skin was dark green and lumpy, like a toad's. Sharp-looking horns jutted from its elbows. I froze. The creature might have been one of those *jinx beasts* my uncle mentioned.

The thing tapped its claws on my box of crayons as it

fed them to Roxy, one at a time. It used to hold 128, but now, only a few colors were left.

I stood still and tried not to make a sound, but I guess it heard me breathing.

Slowly, it turned its head and stared at me with huge eyes. Its pupils were the size of quarters.

Its wet, pig nose glistened.

Its hairy, pointy ears twitched.

"Good luck," the jinx beast whispered. "You'll need it."

The Boogerman

When Sanjay Suda's parents dropped him off at Camp Running Nose, he didn't know what to expect. It turned out to be the most amazing sleepaway camp in the history of the world.

Sanjay joined two hundred other kids as they hiked through woods, rode whitewater rapids, and climbed glaciers. They learned to shoot crossbows and fight with medieval swords. They piloted drones and raced robot ponies. Every kid even got private lessons where they were taught how to carve sculptures with chain saws!

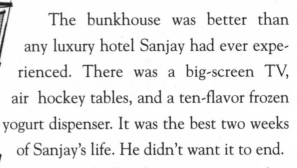

The bunkhouse was better than any luxury hotel Sanjay had ever experienced. There was a big-screen TV, air hockey tables, and a ten-flavor frozen yogurt dispenser. It was the best two weeks of Sanjay's life. He didn't want it to end.

On the final night, everyone stayed up long past dark to roast marshmallows and share stories around a campfire. It was one last fun time together before they all went their separate ways.

As was tradition, all the kids tried to scare each other with the most terrifying and twisted tales they knew.

"Two days ago, I went for a hike in the forest. All. By. Myself," said Connie Jackson, one of the junior counselors sitting next to Sanjay.

While she spoke, she slowly rose to her feet. She kept one hand in her jacket pocket.

"As I went deeper and deeper into the woods, the trees blocked out the sun," she continued. "The air around me grew colder. I shivered, and a chill ran down my spine. Then, when I turned around to head back up the path, I stumbled over a rock. And you'll never guess what I found."

Everyone waited silently.

Connie pulled her hand from her pocket and held up a small red pointy object.

"A rhinoceros pepper!" she told everyone.

"A what?" asked Sanjay, reaching for it. "Let me see."

The girl raised the object over her head so he couldn't grab it.

"A rhinoceros pepper," she repeated. "It's wicked hot,

and *you* don't want to have anything to do with it. Believe me. It'll *kill you*."

Sanjay stared at the red pepper in the girl's hand. It didn't look special or wicked hot or deadly.

"My father is from Thailand and my mother is from India," he told everyone. "We eat spicy food all the time."

"It's not the flavor that'll kill you," Connie replied. "It's . . . *the Boogerman*."

Silence filled the clearing in the woods. Except for the crackling fire, there was no noise. No one made a peep.

Sanjay listened carefully. He wanted to hear more.

"If you find a rhinoceros pepper and it's after midnight, don't sniff it," Connie warned.

Sanjay nodded, a little nervous. It was long past midnight.

"And whatever you do, never whisper the name *Boogerman*," she added.

Sanjay nodded again. He heard a few campers giggling softly, but he ignored them.

"And if you *are* reckless enough to sniff that pepper *and* say that name," Connie continued, "don't ever, ever blow your nose three times and look in a mirror!"

"What?" asked Sanjay. He had to know. "Why not?"

Connie waited for the laughter to die down again.

"A horrible, gooey demon will come for you!" She shouted. "You'll try to get away, but there will be no escape. You will be completely oozed . . . absorbed . . . slimed!"

Sanjay could barely breathe. His knees shook slightly.

"That's not all," said Connie. "It will come for your family and friends, too. No one will be able to stop it. Everyone you know will become a prisoner of goo for all eternity, and it will be your fault. You will have picked your fate!"

"Oh no!" Sanjay shouted. "How could a little red pepper be so dangerous?"

Connie stepped forward.

"Who . . . *nose!*" she shouted as she shoved the red pepper into Sanjay's left nostril.

Startled, he drew in a deep snort, inhaling the pepper farther into his nose.

The campers erupted in laughter.

Sanjay looked around the fire. Kids were laughing . . . and pointing at him.

"Gotcha," said Connie.

The laughter grew louder.

Sanjay felt like a fool. He had fallen for the silliest story of the night. He stood there, with his face nearly as red as the pepper sticking out of his nose.

He had never been more embarrassed in his entire life.

Angrily, Sanjay yanked the pepper from his nostril and shoved it in his pocket. He turned away from the campfire and headed down the twisting path to the bunkhouse.

"Wait!" he heard Connie calling. "I'm sorry. It was just a joke!"

Sanjay didn't turn around. He felt humiliated.

He stomped down the steep hill and through the forest toward the main camp. Along the way, he slipped.

He fell on the muddy, leafy trail. His knees got wet and dirty, but he didn't care. He picked himself up and stumbled onward. He just wanted to go home.

Sanjay kicked open the door to the bunkhouse. The *bang* echoed through the cavernous space. He was alone. Good. He walked into the sparkling white marble bathroom. He'd brush his teeth, then pack his bags, go to sleep, and wait for his parents to pick him up in the morning.

Sanjay's eyes watered from the pepper's heat. He sniffled. His nose burned where the rhinoceros pepper had touched it. He reached for a tissue . . . and blew his nose.

"Ridiculous," he muttered to himself.

He blew his nose a second time . . . and looked in the bathroom mirror.

"Boogerman," he said softly.

Then he blew his nose a third time.

Something in the mirror got his attention. He leaned in for a closer look.

Two globs of snot stuck to the surface of the mirror.

Sanjay stared at the mustard-y splotches.

Suddenly . . . they blinked. Two eyes?

Splish.

Ten glistening dots appeared in a row under them.

Sanjay leaned in to get a closer look . . . and saw that they were moving forward.

Fingertips!

Two greenish-yellow hands reached out of the mirror!

"Garrrr!"

A hideous head with a dozen eyes lurched toward him. Each eyeball twitched and stared at Sanjay from the end of a long, wriggling stalk. The horrible face rippled like a simmering vat of corn chowder.

Hissss!

A rubbery tongue darted from an opening that looked more like a nostril than a mouth. Muck splattered everywhere as the awful shape waggled back and forth, inches from Sanjay's nose.

Sanjay screamed and staggered backward, tripping on the marble strip that ran along the bottom of the doorway. He fell and landed on his butt.

Squoo-oo-oosh!

Frozen with terror, Sanjay watched as a monster gushed from the mirror like two hundred gallons of rancid applesauce! The creature stood at least seven feet tall. It had arms that wriggled in the air like long sticks of mozzarella. Webs of goo stretched between each of its gloppy fingers. Slime rippled over every inch of its gross, oozing body. Grunting and drooling, it lowered its head and leered at Sanjay with all twelve eyes.

"Glorrrrrgh!"

The Boogerman let out a horrible, burbling roar. It sounded like a doomed wooly mammoth sinking into a prehistoric tar pit. Green paste splattered the walls and ceiling of the white marble bathroom.

Sanjay pushed himself up from the floor, turned, and ran. He sprinted through the bunkhouse and scrambled out the front door.

"Help! Help!" he shouted.

No one answered. They were all still far away at the campfire.

"Glorrrrrgh!"

The Boogerman stood in the

bunkhouse doorway and let out another terrifying, syrupy howl.

Sanjay thought about trying to get back to the fire but knew he wouldn't make it up the muddy trail in the dark. Instead, he ran the other way, toward the cluster of buildings that formed the main camp. He could hear the gooey footsteps of the monster squishing on gravel and leaves as it stomped after him.

Sanjay raced to the crossbow shed, pulled open the nearest storage locker, and grabbed a loaded bow. He spun around, took aim, and fired at the oncoming beast.

Splish.

The crossbow bolt hit the Boogerman right between two of its slimy eyestalks . . . and passed right through it! The monster marched forward as if nothing had happened.

Sanjay dropped the crossbow and dashed down the path. He passed the robot pony corral and sped into the medieval weapons armory. His squad had just spent the afternoon practicing hand-to-hand combat, so he knew where to go. He opened a tall cabinet lined with shiny steel weapons and took down a two-handed broadsword.

"Glorrrrrgh!"

The monster sloshed through the armory door.

Slash-flap! Slash-zip! Swish-blap!

Sanjay swung the sword furiously. He slashed and hacked, but he couldn't do any damage to the terrible, gelatinous demon. Wherever the sword cut into gooey, lumpy flesh, it all slid back together as soon as the blade had passed through.

"Glorrrrrgh!"

The Boogerman lashed out with one of its mucus-covered arms. Sanjay jumped back . . . and dropped the sword. It clattered to the floor.

The monster swung its arms twice more. Sanjay dodged both times, then leapt forward and dove between the creature's greasy legs, wincing when his foot bumped against them. He rolled through the armory door, stood up, and ran.

As he raced along the path, Sanjay felt something sticky on his ankle. A blob of green jelly clung to him where he had brushed against the monster. It was crawling up his leg, like an evil slug. He didn't have time to stop and brush it off. He knew the Boogerman was close behind.

In the distance, Sanjay saw something glinting in the moonlight. A chain saw rested against a tree stump. He raced over to it and yanked the power cord.

R-r-r-r-ummmmble!

The heavy-duty gas-powered cutting tool roared to life. Sanjay whirled around and swung with all his might.

R-r-r-r-unnnnch!

The saw's rotating chain tore into the monster's chest, slicing clean through it.

"Glork!" blurted the Boogerman.

The slimy beast stood shaking and flailing its gloopy hands in the air.

Slowly, its sludge-caked torso began to slip backward. It slid from its midsection and fell to the ground, where it burst like a wet bag of moldy green oatmeal.

"I got you," Sanjay panted, triumphant.

He felt the jelly-slug letting go of his leg. It started sliding down to the ground.

Sanjay lowered the chain saw and watched the bottom half of the huge oozing monster. It quivered, struggling to remain on its greasy feet.

"You've been wiped out," he said. "Boogerma—"

Sloosh!

The creature's bottom half gushed upward in a geyser of slime. Glistening coils of goo rose ten feet into the air in a cloud of paste and droplets. The coils fell toward Sanjay and closed around him like wriggling fists.

The chain saw dropped to the ground, and everything . . . went . . . green.

The next morning, Mr. and Mrs. Suda pulled up in front of the main office and waited in their car. Without a word, their son opened the door and climbed into the back seat.

Mrs. Suda smiled in the rearview mirror as she listened for the sound of a clicking seat belt. Then she drove around the circle, out the main gate, and on to the long dirt road that led to the highway.

"Did you have a good two weeks?" Mrs. Suda asked.

No answer.

Mr. Suda glanced over his shoulder. Sanjay sat still with his arms crossed. He stared straight ahead with an odd smile on his face. His skin had a slightly greenish tint.

A drop of slime dangled from his nose.

"Sanjay?" asked Mr. Suda. "Is something wrong?"

His son tilted his head slightly as his smile stretched into a wide, menacing grin. Green goo began to gush from his nose.

"No," he replied in a low, syrupy growl. "It's *snot.*"

Duplicate Release Form

"Sit down, everybody!" Mr. Piper shouted. "Just a little longer. We'll be there in ten minutes."

The crowded school bus sped along Interstate 95 toward the Twin Cities Super Science Center.

Wedged between the window and a fellow fifth grader, Lamar Cooper watched the assistant principal flip through a bundle of green and pink permission slips at the front of the bus. The man's lips moved. Lamar could tell he was counting them carefully.

Thunk!

An empty juice box sailed through the air and bounced off Mr. Piper's shiny head.

"Bull's-eye," Jordan Brown whispered to Lamar.

Lamar would never have chosen to sit next to "Bull's-Eye" Brown. He was trouble. He was probably the worst behaved kid in the school. But it had been the only seat left on the bus. In the end, it was a small price to pay for a trip to the Twin Cities Super Science Center.

Mr. Piper gazed around the bus. Was he looking for the juice box thrower? No, he was counting all the kids. The assistant principal nodded, smiled, and went back to his papers.

Someone tapped Lamar on the shoulder from behind. It was Phoebe Steamer, a girl who was famous for playing pranks. They were never amusing.

"After I finish my sandwich," she said with a mouth full of fried fish and cheese, "want to help me sneak ketchup packets into the bus driver's shoes?"

Lamar shook his head. He hoped she wouldn't do it, and he didn't want to help. He was really looking forward to the Super Science Center. He had heard about it for months, and this was finally his chance to go. The center had everything: rocket-themed roller coasters, laser battles through a human-body-shaped maze, even low-gravity bouncy houses. Ketchup-ing the bus driver's feet would delay their arrival for sure.

"Sit down, Rosa!" Mr. Piper called in a cheerful tone toward the middle of the bus. "And . . . oh, Jimmy. Stop throwing garbage out the window!"

There wasn't a single kid on this bus who Lamar would have wanted on *any* field trip. But his own fourth-grade class wasn't scheduled to visit the Super Science Center. Lamar's class trip was to an apple orchard. Been there.

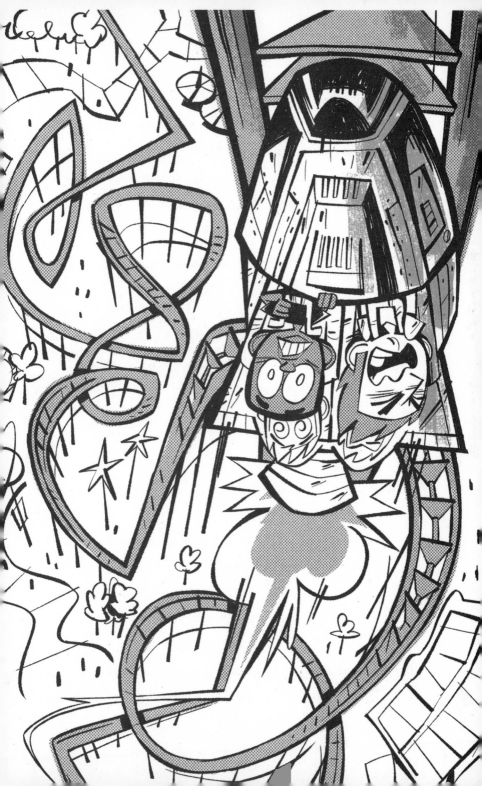

Done that. Boring. Meanwhile, everything he had heard about the Super Science Center sounded awesome. He didn't want to ride in a truck full of hay and spend hours picking straw out of his underwear. He wanted to ride the Venus Volcano Vortex. He didn't want to harvest fruit. He wanted to pick off enemy viruses along the White Blood Cell Combat Corridor.

So when Lamar's class boarded the bus to the orchard, he slipped around the corner and snuck into the line for the bus to the science center.

Scrunch!

Jordan crushed an empty soda can close to Lamar's ear.

"Get ready," Jordan chuckled. "We're about to play a little *brain ball* with Mr. Piper."

Lamar glanced at Mr. Piper's shiny head. It was certainly going to make a good target.

But before any more flying objects could be launched, the assistant principal signaled the driver. The bus rolled off the interstate and onto an access road. A water tower painted to look like a giant magnifying glass rose into the sky.

"Whoa!" someone shouted from a few rows back. "With a magnifier that big, I could fry teachers the way I fry ants!"

Lamar ignored the insect roaster behind him. He was busy gazing through his window into the park.

A high, spinning ride glistened in the late-morning sun. Lamar thought it looked like a giant sunflower. As the bus drew closer, he saw that it was a twirling ring of human-sized test tubes.

"The Centrifuge Screamer," Lamar said softly, watching the tubes whirl faster and faster.

He could see that the people inside were screaming, all right. But he couldn't hear their voices. They must all be sealed tight in their test tubes.

The bus hissed to a stop at the entry gate.

"Listen up, kids," Mr. Piper announced. "Before we can go any farther, I need to make sure we have

all your parents' permission to go on this trip. So please pass me your—"

Splat!

A yogurt cup sailed past him and exploded on the windshield. A glob of white goo landed on the side of Mr. Piper's head.

The assistant principal sighed. Then he reached into his shirt pocket and took out a handkerchief. He wiped away the yogurt and smiled.

"As I was just saying," he continued. "I need to collect any missing permission slips."

Lamar gulped. He was a stowaway on this trip, so he didn't have a Super Science Center permission slip. He was so close, and yet . . .

"I still need forms from two kids," Mr. Piper continued. "Then we can all go into the park and—"

"You can't have mine!" called a girl in the row ahead of Lamar.

It was Isabel Baker. Everyone knew her as Interrupting Izzy. She waved green and pink papers in the air.

"My parents wouldn't sign it," she continued. "They said they didn't want me to get—"

"Come up here right now." Mr. Piper cut her off, looking serious. "Right . . . now!"

Izzy froze, frightened. Then she stood up and walked to the front of the bus. The driver yanked a lever and the door jerked open with a very loud creak.

"You get to spend the day with the guards in the security shed, over there," Mr. Piper told her, pointing to a small windowless building. "We'll pick you up on our way back to school."

A woman outside the shed wore a white hard hat and very bright yellow coveralls with *HOORAY FOR SCIENCE!* printed on the front. She made eye contact with Mr. Piper, and they nodded at each other. Then the woman smiled and began waving at all the kids on the bus.

Izzy stared down at her shoes. She looked like she might cry.

"Hurry up and scram!" someone shouted. "I want to see robot dinosaurs!"

A paper airplane sailed past her and continued out the open door.

Izzy walked slowly down the steps and off the bus.

The assistant principal extended his index finger and took another quick head count. He frowned.

"I'm still missing one permission slip," he called. "If your parents didn't sign, you don't go to the science center."

Lamar groaned quietly. What a complete waste of a day. He lowered his head . . . and spotted something green and pink by his right foot. It was a blank permission slip packet. Izzy must have dropped it on her way off the bus.

Lamar made sure no one was watching. Then he reached down and picked up the papers.

DUPLICATE RELEASE FORM

Full Name of Student:
_____

Parent or Guardian Signature:
_____

Lamar glanced at Jordan. He was busy pulling stuffing from the bus seat and tossing it into the air, paying no attention to anyone.

Lamar squinted at the first paragraph:

My child has permission to enter the Twin Cities Super Science Center and enjoy all the rides and exhibits.

"I need twenty-five signed release forms," Mr. Piper called. "I know how much you all want to see this science center."

Lamar took a pen from his backpack and wrote his name at the top of the page. He used his left hand to sign his dad's name so it didn't look like the same person wrote both. Then he flipped to the second page and did it again.

"Here's my form," Lamar called, standing up and waving the pages in the air. "I meant to give it to you earlier."

Mr. Piper looked relieved. He nodded for Lamar to come forward.

Lamar squeezed past Jordan, marched to the front of the bus, and handed the papers to the assistant principal.

Mr. Piper inspected the green top page. He stared at Lamar for a long moment, then flipped to the second, pink page and studied it, too.

"Well . . . okay," he said slowly.

Lamar grinned. Success! Excited, he turned to head back to his seat.

Mr. Piper tapped him on the shoulder.

"Take this copy," said the assistant principal.

He held out the pink page.

"Put it in your backpack for your parents," he said.

"Yes, sir," said Lamar. "I'll be sure to hand it to them personally as soon as I get home from—"

"Just put it in your backpack," Mr. Piper said quickly. "And go sit down."

Lamar took the pink page and headed back to his seat.

Swick!

Something slimy hit him on the side of his head.

"Spitball fight!" someone yelled.

Soggy wads of chewed-up paper darted around the bus. Lamar held the page in front of his face as a shield as he walked back to his seat. The second paragraph, written in very, very small letters, caught his eye:

My child will go on the DNA Dodge 'Em and the Chromosome Coaster. During the rides, all of my child's body data will be collected so a duplicate can be grown and hatched.

"Duplicate?" Lamar asked himself, puzzled. "Hatched?"

Thump!

An apple core bounced off his shoulder.

"Get out of the way!" someone shouted. "You just cost me two points!"

Lamar wasn't interested in "points" right now. He squinted at the tiny print on the pink paper as he sat down and kept reading.

The duplicate will be identical to my child, with the following exceptions:

I) The duplicate's vocal cords will be much thinner, so it will never be able to speak louder than a gentle whisper.

II) The duplicate will have an obedience amplifier in its brain, so it will always be happy to follow instructions from teachers and parents.

"Carlos and Diane! Stop tossing your shoes at people," Mr. Piper called. He sounded happier now that he had all the permission slips in hand. "You don't want to walk around the science center barefoot, do you?"

The bus began to move again, rolling toward the center's entrance.

Lamar's heart was racing. He kept reading.

While the duplicate is growing, my child will ride the CAT-Scan Slider. My child's memories will be copied and transferred to the duplicate. However, all time-wasting interests and expensive hobbies will be deleted.

"Mr. Piper!" a girl shouted from the back of the bus. "Tommy keeps pulling my hair!"

"She bit me first!" a boy shouted back.

The assistant principal didn't reply. He was smiling and looking out a window. Off in the distance a flag saying SCIENCE SAVES THE DAY! fluttered from a huge tower.

Lamar looked down at the pink paper. This writing was even smaller. He held the paper close to his eyes.

My child will ride the Atom Smasher Speedway and be disintegrated.

The duplicate will be sent home in their place.

Lamar dropped the paper on the floor of the bus and pushed his way up the aisle. Mr. Piper snapped to attention.

"Where do you think you're going?" asked Mr. Piper warily.

"Stop the bus!" Lamar shouted at the bus driver.

Bonk!

Something hard bounced off the back of his head. It was probably one of Carlos's or Diane's shoes. Lamar didn't care. His hands were shaking. He felt his chest tightening. It was getting hard for him to breathe.

"Go back and sit with all your noisy little friends," said Mr. Piper, pointing and grinning.

"No!" shouted Lamar.

He waved at the driver desperately.

"Open the doors! Please!" he begged.

"Relax, dude," said the driver. "I've never heard anyone complain on their way home from this place."

Mr. Piper put a hand on each of Lamar's shoulders.

"Stop! Let go of me!" wailed Lamar. "I wasn't supposed to be on this bus!"

The assistant principal had powerful hands. Lamar couldn't get past him.

"I don't want my interests and hobbies to be deleted!" he screamed. "I don't want to ride the Atom Smasher Speedway!"

"Just have a good time," Mr. Piper said softly in his ear. "It'll be over soon."

"No!" wailed Lamar.

He jerked free and sprinted toward the emergency exit at the back of the bus.

"Food fight!" shouted a girl.

All the kids began tossing half-eaten sandwiches, banana peels, plasticware, and dirty, balled-up napkins. Two kids wrestled on the floor, blocking Lamar's path to the exit.

The bus passed under a huge, shiny orange banner:

SPRING SPECIAL!

TWO FOR THE PRICE OF ONE!

"Everyone!" Lamar screamed. "You've got to listen to me!"

No one listened. They had begun to sing. It was much, much louder than a gentle whisper.

"Ninety-nine bottles of pop on the wall. Ninety-nine bottles of pop . . ."

"Don't get off the bus! Don't go into the center!" Lamar shouted desperately. "Your parents all signed *duplicate release forms*!"

Dog Years

Lydia Grisham was late again.

She had a math test in five minutes, and the front entrance to Pavlov Elementary School was still four blocks away.

If she wasn't in her chair when the test started, she'd get another zero. Combined with her other two, that would be her third zero. And three zeros make a minus.

Lydia didn't care about math, but her parents had warned her. If she got any more minuses, they'd start taking away the things she *did* care about: food and friends. The pizza party she had coming up on Saturday? Lydia cared! Her rainbow sparkle sneakers slapped the pavement. She ran as fast as she could.

In the distance, she saw that the side door to the cafeteria was propped open. She could cut through and just reach her classroom in time. But someone was in her way. An old man stood in the middle of the sidewalk holding a leash, watching something on the ground.

"Coming through!" she called, racing toward him.

The man looked up but did not move.

"Get out of the way!" shouted Lydia.

At the last second, she swerved around him, kept going and—

Thump!

Her foot hit something small and soft.

Lydia froze. She looked down. A tiny dog lay on the grass next to the sidewalk, whimpering. It might have been a puppy, or maybe it was just a really small dog. A wiener dog or terrier or whatever. Luckily, it didn't seem to have been hurt. It whimpered once more, then sniffed at a blade of grass in front of its long fuzzy nose.

"Hey, mister," Lydia told the man. "I really didn't mean to . . ."

Her voice trailed off.

The man wasn't listening. He was watching his dog.

She followed the man's gaze. A few flecks of rainbow sparkle glitter twinkled where Lydia's shoe had accidently hit the animal.

When she looked up again, the man was glaring at her.

"I-I'm sorry," said Lydia. "I was in a hurry. There's a big important test, and I—"

The old man grabbed her sleeve.

"Dog years," he whispered.

"What?" asked Lydia.

"Dog . . . years," he said again, slowly and very quietly.

The man let go of her sleeve. Then he knelt and flipped the dog back onto its stubby legs. He patted it on its head and stood up again, holding its leash.

Without another word, the man and the dog turned and headed off into the field.

Lydia watched them trudge into the distance.

Bing-bing-bing! Bing-bing-bing!

Her phone's alarm sounded. She didn't have time to think about this strangeness. She had less than a minute to get to the math test. Lydia shrugged and sped off to school.

She reached her seat just in time to pick up a pencil, and answered the last question just before the end-of-class bell rang.

As she turned in her paper, Lydia finally relaxed. New minus? No. New pizza party? Yes!

She felt triumphant the rest of the day. By the time she headed home, she had forgotten all about the odd man and his wiener dog or terrier or whatever.

The next morning, Lydia woke up feeling strange. She couldn't quite figure it out. There was nothing exactly wrong that she could describe, but things seemed different somehow. On the walk to school, her rainbow sparkle sneakers didn't feel like they fit right. They seemed to have gotten tighter overnight.

When she reached her locker, her hall neighbor Cassie pointed at her feet.

"What?" Lydia asked. "Do you see something wrong with my shoes?"

"No." Cassie chuckled. "But I can see your *somebody loves me* socks."

Lydia looked down. A row of red hearts peeked from the gap between her jean cuffs and the tops of her sneakers. The words *somebody*, *loves*, and *me* were written in hearts, fully visible.

She blushed. Those socks were a holiday gift from her aunt. They were embarrassing. Lydia never would have worn them if she'd known anybody was going to see. Had her pants shrunk in the wash? All day at school, she tugged at her jeans, trying to keep the socks hidden.

By the end of the week, her parents had noticed changes, too. Lydia's clothes weren't getting smaller. Lydia was growing!

"Where's the flood?" Mr. Grisham asked as Lydia passed him on her way through the kitchen.

"I'll take you to get new pants after school," said Mrs. Grisham.

"Thanks, Mom," said Lydia. "I need new rainbow sparkle sneakers, too. These are too small for me."

She quickly grew taller. By the end of the month, Lydia was the tallest kid in fifth grade. Suddenly, everyone wanted her on their basketball and volleyball teams. Lydia was flattered, but she didn't like the idea of scuffing up her sneakers.

"I think we should make a doctor's appointment for you," her mother said one afternoon. "You're growing like a teenager. They should take some tests, just in case there's anything that we—"

"No!" Lydia interrupted. "No! No! No! I don't like tests. They're not fair, and I don't need any! You always make me do things I don't want to! Do I have to tell you everything? Nobody listens to me in this house. Parents are so stupid!"

"Are you sure you're still ten years old?" asked her father. "You're really starting to sound like a teenager."

Soon other people started thinking Lydia was a teenager, too.

She went to the movies with her friends, but the usher wouldn't allow her in with a kid's ticket.

"If you're thirteen or older, you've got to pay full price," said the usher.

Lydia tried to explain that she was ten, but he didn't believe her. She didn't have any extra money, so she had to go home alone.

A few weeks later, her family went out to eat at their favorite restaurant.

"Why is this place suddenly more expensive?" asked Mrs. Grisham when the check arrived.

"It's the same prices as always," the waiter answered.

"What happened to the kids-eat-free special?" asked Mr. Grisham.

"Sorry," said the waiter. "That deal's only for kids twelve and under."

A week later, Lydia's mom took her to replace her rainbow sparkle sneakers for the third time that year.

"I can't help you anymore," said the clerk at the shoe store. "They only make that style for kids, not teenagers."

Now Lydia's parents really began to worry. They tried to convince her to see a doctor, but Lydia was not interested.

"Doctors don't know anything!" she snapped at them. "They're like teachers with lab coats. They just want to sell you some medicine. Then they try to scare you with stories about kids getting big and not listening to grown-ups, blah, blah, blah, blah, blah."

That night, Lydia glanced in the mirror while brushing her teeth. She spotted two small puffy red dots on her upper lip.

"Zits?" She gasped.

She had been happy to grow taller. She didn't mind people thinking she was older. She had no problem asking her parents for extra money to pay for bus rides, and museum tickets, and admission to the zoo. But Lydia was *not* ready to start worrying about acne!

PSST! HOLD THIS PICTURE TO BRIGHT LIGHT

That night, she had a dream she was brushing her teeth again. She put down her toothbrush and leaned in to inspect her face.

This time, instead of acne, patches of stiff, long black hairs had sprouted on either side of her lip and around her cheeks.

"Whiskers?" she asked.

Lydia stared at the hair. When she took a step back and gazed in the mirror once more, her whole face had changed! Long, thin whiskers dangled from her cheeks. Her skin was blanketed with brown and tan fur. In

place of her mouth, a large, wet nose sniffed and twitched on the end of a snout. She sported a pair of long floppy ears.

The dog-girl in the mirror slowly opened its jaws and howled. A long, wavering, hound-like howl . . . and Lydia woke up!

"What a horrible dream," she panted, sitting up in bed.

She ran to her parents' bedroom and told them she was ready to see a doctor immediately.

The next day . . . tests began.

There were blood tests, eye tests, and hearing tests. Experts weighed Lydia and measured her arms and legs and even the length of her ears.

One doctor sent her to a clinic to get a personality test. The results said that Lydia liked food and friends but didn't care about grades.

"Did someone get paid to write this report?" asked Lydia's dad.

A week later, they found the right specialist.

Rebecca Kent, MD, had an advanced medical degree,

plus degrees in teenage psychology, sports medicine, and canine biology.

"I've read about this condition," Dr. Kent told the Grishams. "Your daughter has a case of hundejahre."

"Hoon-dee what?" asked Lydia's mom.

"It's pronounced *hoon-deh-yah-ruh*," the doctor said again slowly. "That's German for 'dog years.'"

"Dog years," Lydia repeated quietly. Where had she heard that before?

All at once, it came back to her. She had forgotten about the old man and his wiener dog or terrier or whatever. She had never mentioned it to her parents.

"She's aging rapidly," Dr. Kent continued. "According to my estimates, about fifteen times the normal rate."

"Fifteen?" asked Lydia's father. "I thought a single dog year was equal to *seven* human years."

"A lot of people believe that, but it's actually more complicated," the doctor replied. "The rate depends on the type of dog and whether it's an adult or a puppy."

Lydia tried to picture the little dog she had accidentally kicked. Was it a puppy? Was it a really old dog?

"What could have caused this?" asked Mrs. Grisham.

"I hope it's not contagious," said Mr. Grisham.

"I hope you have enough money to pay my fees," said Dr. Kent.

Lydia looked back and forth between the grown-ups but said nothing.

"We may never know how she got it," said the doctor. "What's important is that we take control of it before she gets too old."

"I've always said kids grow up too fast these days," said Lydia's father.

"This is serious," said Lydia's mother.

"If we don't correct this, your daughter's body will be sixty years old before she starts high school," said Dr. Kent.

Dog to human years
FORMULA

DOG AGE =

A × ln (HUMAN AGE) + B

"Sixty!" wailed Lydia. "And I still won't have a driver's license."

"How can we, um, cure this?" asked Mrs. Grisham.

"Wait here," said the doctor, opening the door to a hallway. "I have a special cabinet for rare and unusual conditions in the back room."

She left and closed the door behind her.

Lydia and her parents stood in the room and silently waited.

"There's a box of your grandmother's old dresses in the attic," said Mr. Grisham.

"What?" asked Lydia.

"I think your father was trying to make a joke, dear," said her mother.

"Well, it wasn't funny," said Lydia.

"Kibble!" announced the doctor, pushing open the door.

She stepped back into the room and dropped a stack of folders on her desk.

"Change what she eats and her body will change how she ages," she said.

"What she eats?" asked Mrs. Grisham.

"Yes," said Doctor Kent. "Replace everything with dog food."

"*Dog* food?" asked Lydia.

"Exactly," replied the doctor. "Her human blood cells will begin to miss the flavors and nutrients from the kinds of food that human kids eat. Over time, her body will wake up to the fact that she's not a dog."

Lydia felt queasy.

"I can get food from that pet store near our house," said Mr. Grisham. "They have dozens of varieties, including some vegan, gluten-free options. And some food for really old dogs, too. "

Lydia couldn't tell if her father was trying to be funny or not.

"Introduce it to her slowly, though," Dr. Kent warned. "Switching from candy and ice cream to ground lamb, tuna, and liver is a big shock to the system."

Lydia's parents nodded.

"Stick with this program for two months," said the doctor.

OLD FELLER

BEST FOOD
FOR DOGS
CLOSE TO
DEATH

"Months?" asked Lydia, horrified.

The doctor nodded and pushed the folders around on her desk.

"*People* months," said Dr. Kent.

"We'll do it," Mrs. and Mr. Grisham said at the same time.

"We?" asked Lydia. "*You* don't have to eat dog food."

"And keep her away from other kids," the doctor added. "We don't know what caused this, and we don't want it to spread."

April and May were the longest months ever.

Lydia stayed home from school and attended classes on her laptop. She missed out on parties, playgrounds, and concerts. She missed two field trips, and the spring carnival, too.

Her shoes and her pants always felt tight. It was annoying, but at least it reminded her to stick with the program.

That, of course, meant the *diet*.

For the first few days, Lydia sprinkled dog kibble on slices of pizza and tossed it with bowls of spaghetti. It wasn't half bad. She pretended the little crunchy lumps were croutons or bits of tortilla chips. She decided the ones shaped like gray bones were the best of the bunch, followed by the ones shaped like red fish. The blue diamonds were just so-so.

After a week, her parents took away all people food. They just gave her a bowl of dog food three times daily.

"Doctor's orders," her mother reminded her.

Lydia didn't like it at all, but she stuck with it. As she ate, she pictured herself graduating from high school, wearing one of her grandmother's old dresses at the ceremony. That made it easier to keep chewing.

By the end of the first month, her mom started pouring warm water over the food. Every meal turned into a bowl of slippery brown sludge.

"Mom!" Lydia wailed. "This is disgusting!"

"Read the bag," said Mrs. Grisham. "It says 'gravy brings out the flavor dogs crave.'"

"I'm not a dog!" snapped Lydia.

"Then don't bark at me," said her mother. "Stop growling and eat."

Two months later, they went back to see Dr. Kent.

"Good news," she announced, waving a sheet of test results. "Lydia's cells think she's a normal human girl again. She's back to people years."

"Wonderful," said Mrs. Grisham.

"That's cause for a celebration," said Mr. Grisham. "Let's plan a pizza party."

"You'd better hold off on that," Dr. Kent warned. "We don't want a relapse."

"We?" snapped Lydia. "You said *we* again! I haven't seen anyone else eating dog food recently."

"Does she have to keep on the special diet?" asked Lydia's mother.

"Definitely," said the doctor. "Keep the kibble coming for the rest of the summer."

"Does she need to stay away from other kids, too?" asked Mr. Grisham.

"No," said the doctor. "She can leave the house and be around others, just as long as she sticks to dog food."

Lydia perked up at that. At last, she was going to be outside.

On the car ride home, her mind filled with thoughts of running, playing ball, and seeing her friends. She couldn't wait to go to the park and catch up on everything she had missed. She opened the window, poked her head out, and let the wind rush across her face. It felt great.

"I'm off to the park," Lydia announced as they pulled into the driveway.

"Come inside and have some lunch before you go," said her mother.

Lydia trotted after her into the kitchen.

"Awww," she whimpered as she dug among the bags of dog chow in the pantry. "There's nothing left but peas and mackerel."

"Don't worry," said her mother. "I sent your dad to pick up some more tripe-and-beef-kidney combo mix."

"Yum!" said Lydia.

"I asked him to grab a can of the new fermented salmon in pickled seaweed for you, too," Mrs. Grisham added.

"That sounds delicious, Mom," said Lydia.

Her stomach rumbled. It was well past her feeding time, and she was thirsty, too. She scampered upstairs to the bathroom. She flipped up the toilet seat, knelt down, and began to lap up the water.

"Lydia!" her mother called from downstairs. "Your father is back. He's got chicken-liver-and-bison-heart blend!"

Lydia raised her head. Her favorite!

"I'll be there in a minute, Mom!" she called, and went back to drinking from the toilet.

Epizeuxis

"Reading is boring," moaned Naomi. "It's incredibly, incredibly, *incredibly* boring."

"Twenty minutes," Rudy groaned as he stared at the clock on the library wall. "We've only been here for twenty minutes."

"I hate, hate, hate books," said Margaret.

"And *I* hate, hate, hate, hate libraries," said Sasha.

"Shhhh!" said Ms. Milliron, the new replacement librarian, from her desk.

A few days ago, Naomi, Rudy, Margaret, and Sasha had all agreed it would be funny to tip over a bookshelf. They snuck into the school library while the kindergarteners were having story time. Then they all pushed really hard on NONFICTION A TO F until it toppled. Books flew everywhere, the little kids screamed and cried, and Mr. Peterson, the librarian, squawked like a hysterical chicken as he scrambled around, trying to keep the books and shelves in place.

It was hilarious.

Unfortunately, the prank had worked *too* well. When the big shelf came down, it bumped the one behind it, and that shelf bumped another, and another, and so on. A dozen bookshelves fell like dominos.

Naomi, Rudy, Margaret, and Sasha still thought it was hilarious. But then an old, heavy dictionary had landed on Mr. Peterson's head. He went to the hospital, and the four of them were sentenced to a month of *book detention*. And *that* wasn't hilarious at all!

Now they sat around an extra-low table that was meant for little kids, with a big stack of books in the center. No phones and no talking, only silent reading in the library for four hours a day.

Tick. Tick. Tick.

Ms. Milliron clicked her pen three times to get everyone's attention.

"I couldn't help overhearing your conversation," she said. "We all know you're not supposed to talk during detention."

She put down her pen and rose from her chair.

CLICK!
CLICK!
CLICK!

"But . . . it did make me think of something *interesting*," she said.

"Yawn!" blurted Naomi.

"Twenty-two minutes," said Rudy.

Ms. Milliron walked around her desk with an eager smile on her face. If she heard Naomi's and Rudy's comments, she didn't show it.

"Would you like to add an unusual word to your vocabulary?" she asked.

"Not really," Sasha replied.

"Really, *really* not really," said Margaret.

Ms. Milliron stopped close to their table.

"When you repeat a word or a phrase several times, it's called an epizeuxis," she explained, still smiling.

Margaret looked at Rudy and rolled her eyes.

"*E . . . pih . . . zook . . . sis,*" the replacement librarian repeated slowly.

"Is that a real word?" asked Naomi.

"It is," replied Ms. Milliron. "Say something more than once for extra emphasis and it's an epizeuxis."

"That's *kind* of interesting," admitted Rudy. "But what happens if you say 'epizeuxis' a bunch of times?"

Ms. Milliron froze. She suddenly looked worried.

"I—I don't think you should," she said.

The kids all glanced at each other.

"Epizeuxis, epizeuxis," Sasha said quickly.

"Stop that," said Ms. Milliron. "I'm serious."

"Epizeuxis, epizeuxis, epizeuxis," said Margaret, louder.

"Please!" Ms. Milliron shouted, waving her hands frantically. "You don't know what you're doing!"

"E-pi-zeu-xis," Naomi called in a singsong voice. "E-pi . . ."

Boom!

A fiery explosion erupted beside Ms. Milliron, knocking her to the floor.

The library's five windows shattered at the same time. A dark, sooty cloud rolled through the room. It smelled like a burnt Pop-Tart someone had forgotten in the toaster.

Slowly, the smog cleared, revealing a colossal creature over eight feet tall. A giant green half-human, half-lizard beast with two legs and four arms. Its huge, frowning mouth took up more than half its face, and instead of a nose and eyes, it had three more mouths. Its limbs were dotted with quivering pink oval shapes that looked like mouths, too.

"I AM EPIZEUXIS!" it roared. "WHO DARES AWAKEN ME FROM MY SLUMBER?"

As it spoke, all the lips on its arms and legs twitched, as if speaking along with the booming voice.

"This is not my fault," Ms. Milliron whimpered from the floor. "Really, really . . ."

The creature swept its head back and forth, as if trying to figure out who had spoken. Then it crouched over her.

"I WARNED YOU TO STOP TELLING PEOPLE ABOUT THAT WORD, NANCY!" it thundered.

All of the creature's lips clamped shut, except for the openings in place of its eyes. They stretched into wide circles.

"Wait!" wailed the replacement librarian.

Gushhhhhh!

A stream of mustard-gray mist began to spray from the openings. It rained down on Ms. Milliron, coating her with a layer of bubbling foam.

"No, no, no!" she shouted.

Sizzle!

The replacement librarian dissolved, sloshing into a puddle on the floor like six gallons of butterscotch pudding.

Zip!

A long white tube stretched out from the mouth where the creature's nose should have been. It looked like a giant hollow noodle, dangling over the sludge that used to be Ms. Milliron.

Slur-r-r-p!

The monster sucked up the goo. In less than a minute, it was all gone.

The kids stood there in shock. Nobody moved.

"That's really disgusting," Sasha whispered to Rudy. "And I mean really, really, really, really—"

"SILENCE!" Epizeuxis commanded. "YOU HAVE INTERRUPTED, INTERRUPTED, AND INTERRUPTED MY SLUMBER! NOW YOU MUST FACE THE CONSEQUENCES!"

The beast raised all four arms and pointed a leathery index finger at each of the students.

"YOUR NEXT WORDS . . . WILL BE YOUR LAST WORDS!" it roared, standing up again.

All of its mouths opened and took a deep breath at the same time.

Whoosh!

In a flash, the terrible thing vanished.

"It's gone," said Naomi.

"That sure was creepy," said Rudy.

"And so gross," Margaret added.

"Holy schna-moley," Sasha whispered.

The school security guard, Officer Cowen, was chatting with the basketball coach and a few players when he heard an explosion coming from inside the school.

"Wait here," he told them, and headed around the corner to investigate.

The security guard followed a strange smell and spotted smoke coming from the library. Cautiously, he pushed open the door and entered.

The library was a wreck. Broken glass and books were everywhere. Four kids stood around a table, looking stunned.

"Is everyone okay?" he asked.

"It's gone," said Naomi.

"What's gone?" asked Officer Cowen. "Where?"

"That sure was creepy," said Rudy.

"What's this stuff?" the security guard asked, pointing to mustard-gray splotches on the carpet.

"And so gross," Margaret added.

"Holy schna-moly," Sasha whispered.

Officer Cowen glanced around the room. Every window had been shattered. There was no sign of the replacement librarian.

"What happened in here?" he asked.

"It's gone," said Naomi.

"Where's Ms. Milliron?" he asked.

"That sure was creepy," said Rudy.

The security guard scratched his head.

"What's gotten into you kids?" he asked,

"And so gross," said Margaret.

"Holy schna-moley," said Sasha.

Officer Cowen asked them a dozen more questions.

It looked like the kids were trying to answer, but they kept using the same words over and over, no matter what he said.

Those words were their last words. They were the only ones they would ever say again.

SPECIAL BONUS PREVIEW!

An exclusive sample from the soon-to-be-released, 847-page nature guidebook

Think Twice Before You Go Outside!

by R.U. Ginns

Chapter Sixteen

The Deadly Birds of North America

Few activities are as terrifying as leaving your home to visit nature. Still, there are some reckless people who do this often, and bird-watching is a very popular hobby. What few "birders" realize, however, is that while we have been watching the birds, they have also been watching us!

Today's birds are the descendants of the mighty dinosaurs. Yes, these creatures' ancestors once ruled the entire planet. They terrorized and towered over all other living things.

But then, suddenly, the largest dinosaurs all died out. Only small, feathered dinosaurs remained. Over time, they became *birds*.

That's when mammals took over. As you can probably understand, this annoyed the birds. Even worse, *human* mammals put up buildings. And most buildings have windows. Windows that birds smack into all the time.

Each time a bird smacks into a window, or gets chased by a house cat, or is forced to beg for bread crumbs in a park, the birds are reminded of how low they have sunk.

Their mighty ancestors struck fear in the hearts of everyone, and they ate what they wanted. Now birds must fight with rats and squirrels for stale seeds in a bird feeder!

But, day by day, they have been plotting their revenge.

Keep this chapter handy. If it came as a special bonus preview in another book, you might want to separate the pages to keep in your pocket at all times. You should be very grateful that you can read this exclusive sample for free, and that you got it *without having to go outside.*

Memorize all these important facts. They may save your life someday.

Stork

Storks are large carnivores with six-foot wingspans.

For some reason, there are dozens of stories about how storks deliver babies to happy new parents. Nothing could be further from the truth. If you see a stork circling in the sky, it is probably because it has spotted a new baby below and is planning to snatch it.

Most storks would happily gobble up a baby whose parents aren't paying attention. The bird's enormous bill and throat pouch amplify sound, so you would be able to hear for miles the pitiful cries of the infant as the stork sailed off into the clouds.

Hummingbird

Hummingbirds have a dozen wings, but they keep all but two of them tucked under their feathers most of the time. If you ever frighten a hummingbird, it will begin to flap all twelve wings at once in an attempt to terrify you.

Believe me, it works!

These nectar-drinkers are fascinated by ears.

If you ever get a chance to observe one up close, you'll probably notice that it is buzzing around constantly. As it hovers, it is working up the courage to slip its long pointy beak into your ear, all the way to your brain. Then you would be helpless as the bird sucked your brain until your skull was a hollow shell.

Never fall asleep outside. Hummingbirds will not be able to resist!

OWL

Owls have keen night vision. They also have powerful hearing. That means when you're out in the dark, they know exactly where you are and what you are doing.

They share information with each other, and keep track of everything you have ever said about birds, and the number of chicken sandwiches you have eaten.

Owls are highly intelligent. They understand how much work it is for a medium-sized bird to kill a full-sized human. Fortunately (for owls), their sharp senses help them identify your most vulnerable areas, such as the base of your skull and that small indentation in the middle of your upper lip.

Most owls are not interested in eating you, only mortally wounding you and watching you die.

Penguin

Penguins love to snap at the toes and fingers of any human foolish enough to swim in their path. Then they happily float away and watch with glee as the blood draws the attention of nearby sharks.

Penguins enjoy watching people getting torn to pieces by sharks the way humans enjoy watching funny cat videos.

You may have heard that penguins are flightless birds. That's not true. Penguins *can* fly. They simply choose not to do it. There are too many beaches filled with frolicking humans to waste time flapping their wings.

Crow

A flock of crows is called a "murder," and that makes a lot of sense. Crows are experts at balancing on high-voltage power lines. They know how dangerous electricity is to humans, so it gives these birds a lot of satisfaction to sit around on something so deadly to their enemies.

When you see a crow perched up high, it is natural to think it is covered with dark feathers. But they are not feathers at all. Never touch them!

Crows' bodies are made entirely of sticky goo. If you make the mistake of touching one, it will stick to your hand and it will be almost impossible to remove.

If you see someone wearing mittens or a knit cap during the summer, it's probably because they have a crow stuck to them and they can't get it loose, so they're wearing something to cover it up.

Nobody knows how blobby, oily, gooey crows are able to fly.

Again, never touch a crow. Or a chicken sandwich.

Starling

These birds gather in groups by the thousands and fly in spectacular flocks called murmurations.

Bird experts have calculated that a person standing in the middle of a murmuration could have every last ounce of their flesh stripped clean, right down to the skeleton, in fifteen seconds.

Note: If you are interested in a career as a scientist, do not become a bird flock calculator. That job is dangerous and does not pay well.

Mockingbird

These fierce birds defend their nests from all enemies, even from grizzly bears. So don't think *you* scare them one bit!

Mockingbirds' heads are located at their rear. If you think you are looking at a mockingbird's face, you are actually staring at its butt. They have a fake beak and a pair of eye-shaped nodes that are meant to confuse you. This will cost you several precious seconds that you should be using to run for your life!

Most mockingbirds won't try to kill a human directly. That would be too easy. Instead, they use their songs to confuse humans and cause them to walk into a busy highway, off a cliff, or into the path of a large approaching starling murmuration.

Magpie

The magpie is a clever bird that collects all kinds of objects. This includes shiny coins, bits of colorful paper, and human ears. To harvest its treasures, the magpie uses a pair of wormlike tentacles located between its chin and chest. It keeps them coiled at all times, ready to reach out and snatch something.

What these birds truly crave, however, is your *uvula*. That's the fleshy little knob that hangs at the back of your throat. If you see a magpie cocking its head and looking at you, it is probably calculating the best flight path into your mouth, where it plans to wrap its tentacles around your uvula, pluck it free, and fly away.

Turkey

You've probably heard someone say that a turkey goes *gobble, gobble.* That's a common mistake. Turkeys go *hiss* right before they *gobble you!*

Hidden between their tail feathers, turkeys have a row of flexible blades. They are razor sharp, and can spin like a food processor. If someone tells you they are bringing a turkey to your Thanksgiving dinner, you'd better hope it is not a live one, or you'll be cleaning up bloodstains until the middle of December!

When they get together in private, scientists refer to turkeys as "splatterbirds." But don't bother trying to get any scientists to admit that. They hope that if they keep the name secret, then the turkeys won't hunt them down and dice them.

Indigo Bunting

Many bird lovers are fascinated by the indigo bunting's ability to remember thousands of complicated songs.

Buntings also remember the names and addresses of thousands of people who have attacked, annoyed, or offended them. They never forget a face, and they are always plotting their revenge!

The revenge may come in the form of a peck or scratch loaded with deadly poison. Buntings also like to sabotage car brakes and slice elevator cables.

When the ambulance arrives, who could suspect that sweet little bird, minding its own business, singing one of a thousand cheerful songs?

I hope this chapter has succeeded in warning you about some of the dangerous creatures that are hovering nearby. Maybe even over your head right now. Personally, whenever I have to say the word *birds*, I put a little extra emphasis on the *r*, and I tremble a little, as if I am shivering, so it comes out "Bir-r-r-rds."

You try it:

Birds. Bir-r-r-r-rds.

Now, think twice before you go outside!

—R.U. GINNS

Construct-a-Bot

Tyler Brown made sure to arrive at the party early. This wasn't just any old birthday—this was a special occasion.

It was a Jeremy Aggleton birthday party.

Tyler had heard all about them for years, but he had never been to one. Not until today. And he didn't want to miss any of it.

Everybody knew Jeremy Aggleton had amazing parties. They had wicked interactive games, the best food, the latest videos, and the most awesome party favors.

Last year, kids at school talked for weeks about Jeremy's eleventh birthday party and the incredible interstellar celebration he threw. Jeremy's parents decorated the lobby of their condominium to look like a space station. Caterers, dressed like astronauts, served rocket hot dogs and flying-saucer hamburgers. A DJ in an alien costume played dance music with sci-fi sound effects. The holographic planetarium moon bounce could hold forty kids at a time. Everyone took home laser-guided drones and candy that made their teeth glow in the dark for weeks after they ate it.

Tyler didn't really like Jeremy. But he felt very left out that he hadn't been invited.

So he made a vow: he'd do everything possible to get invited to the next Jeremy Aggleton party.

Jeremy was annoying, and all he ever talked about was himself and his super-rich parents. He didn't care about school either, at least not as much as most of Tyler's friends. But Tyler really wanted an invitation, so he had gone to great lengths to convince Jeremy that they were pals.

Tyler let Jeremy join his *Base Battle Blaster* platoon, even though Jeremy was a below-average gamer. Jeremy

almost never helped the team win. Tyler knew the only reason Jeremy racked up kills at all was because his parents had bought him a top-of-the-line gaming computer. If Tyler had parents who bought *him* a machine with a force-feedback controller, he'd totally rule *Base Battle Blaster*. And every other video game, for that matter.

Tyler persuaded the robotics team to let Jeremy join, even though he wasn't good at planning, designing, or 3D printing anything.

He even helped Jeremy with programming homework every Wednesday. That was the least fun of all. Jeremy didn't understand half of the simplest coding concepts. It was a slog, but at last, it was all going to be worth it.

The party was about to start.

Tyler's parents had dropped him off outside the gate

at 200 Eisenhower Center. Now he headed to the security booth, clutching in his hand the invitation Jeremy had given him. LED lights on the card flashed the words *Jeremy Turns Twelve! A Mystery Surprise Celebration.*

There was no one at the booth to show the invitation to. The sun had started going down, and it was dark. Farther down the drive, Tyler saw an empty parking lot and an enormous warehouse building with all the lights off.

Tyler smiled. Mystery parties and escape rooms were his kind of fun.

He reached the dark building. This was definitely mysterious. He didn't hear music or party sounds coming from inside, and there were no balloons or signs of a celebration.

The only light came from a small box beside a pair of glass doors. A narrow screen glowed on a keypad.

Tyler glanced at the invitation again. There wasn't a security code or any kind of password included on it. He squinted at the blinking card for a while, trying to spot any sort of hidden message.

Nothing. Had Jeremy forgotten to include the code?

Tyler shrugged it off. Numerical passwords weren't that tough. He could usually

crack one in less than a minute. He began entering numbers. Four digits. Five digits. Six digits.

Okay. This one was tough. Whoever set it up knew what they were doing. And it certainly was a lot of security just for a one-night birthday party. He kept typing.

Ten minutes later, the terminal coughed it up. Tyler entered the correct eight digits, the keypad beeped, and the doors swung open.

Tyler expected flashing lights, or the sound of a DJ or a band playing.

Nope. Silence.

Tyler sniffed. No cake, candles, or cotton candy. It smelled like motor oil and burning rubber.

He stepped into a square chamber about ten feet across. The entire back wall was a corrugated metal door, the kind you'd see on a garage. To the left, a touch screen bathed the room in blue light. It looked like a bank machine.

He walked to the terminal and tapped the screen. Two choices appeared:

COLLECT ROBOT

RETURN ROBOT

Tyler's heart leapt in excitement. This wasn't a mystery party after all. It was a robot party!

All those hours pleading with his friends to let Jeremy join their hackathon were finally going to pay off. He pressed Collect Robot.

SELECT ROBOT TYPE

Tyler wondered if he would get to keep his robot as a party favor. He remembered hearing about Jeremy's ninth birthday. It had been a dungeon adventure party where everyone got to build their own stuffed magical creature. A kid showed up at school the next day dragging a life-sized three-headed dragon with eyes that lit up when you pulled its tail.

Robots were much cooler than dragons.

He studied the choices on the screen.

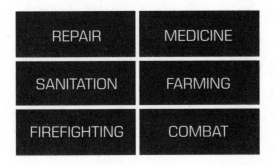

REPAIR	MEDICINE
SANITATION	FARMING
FIREFIGHTING	COMBAT

Tyler wasn't sure why anyone would want a sanitation robot when they could choose firefighting or combat.

This was going to be amazing, but . . . where was everyone else? Tyler knew of at least three other kids invited to the party. Could they all be running late?

Whatever, he thought. *You snooze, you lose.* Tyler wasn't going to wait around for other kids to show up and claim all the best robots.

He tapped the Combat button.

The screen flashed twice and a message appeared.

WARNING: COMBAT ROBOTS ARE ONLY
FOR HIGHLY TRAINED INDIVIDUALS.

Many pictures of robots appeared on the screen. Some had wheels. Others had treads like a tank. One had skis.

Tyler chose one with mechanical legs.

A video began to play. A 3D animation of the robot moved across the screen. It smashed through a wall, kicking things out of the way, and stomped up and over a pile of bricks and twisted metal.

ENTER YOUR LICENSE KEY
TO VERIFY WEAPONS SELECTION

Weapons. This was getting good.

Tyler began typing again. If he could crack the front-door code, he could figure out the key for weapons.

As he worked, he marveled at the advanced puzzles. It was pretty high-level logic for a party, especially one for a kid like Jeremy, who needed help just to pass a basic programming class. Then again, maybe the messages were

customized for every guest. Maybe Jeremy was trying to impress Tyler with a tough code to crack.

Not that anything Jeremy could do was going to impress Tyler.

Finally, the screen beeped.

SELECT WEAPONS

A long list of choices appeared on the screen. Tyler tapped everything that sounded awesome.

ROCKET LAUNCHER

SONIC BRAIN MELTER

SAW BLADES

NUCLEAR SELF-DESTRUCT SEQUENCE

It didn't matter if any of his real friends were going to be at the party. Tyler was going home with the best robot toy ever. And then he wouldn't have to talk to Jeremy Aggleton again. At least, not until next year's birthday came around.

He reviewed his choices. A toy robot that could launch rockets and melt brains with sonic weapons would be awesome. He pictured himself playing with it, slicing up pretend enemies with its spinning blades until it blew itself up with a massive atomic explosion.

ASSEMBLING ROBOT
PLEASE STAND BY

Tyler's phone rang.

He took it out of his pocket. Jeremy's name flashed on the screen. Tyler accepted the call.

"What's taking you so long?" the voice on the phone chirped. "You're missing all the fun stuff. Everyone's already put on their trench coats and their sunglasses. We're passing out mystery milkshakes and getting ready to hear our undercover identities."

"Undercover identities?" asked Tyler. "What are you talking about?"

"For my super-investigator hero party," said Jeremy. "You're gonna miss me cutting crimefighter code cake."

"Crimefighter code cake?" asked Tyler. "I'm building a—"

"The detective dance troop is arriving," Jeremy interrupted.

"I don't understand," said Tyler. "I'm choosing features for my robot."

"Robot? What are you talking about?" asked Jeremy. "Where are you?"

"I'm in the lobby," he answered. "Two Hundred Eisenhower Center."

"Oh, that explains it," said Jeremy. "People make that mistake all the time. My condo is at 200 Eisenhower *Terrace*."

"Terrace?" Tyler replied, glancing at the blinking invitation in his hand.

"The building at Eisenhower Center is some kind of factory," said Jeremy. "They've got lots of security."

"Factory?" asked Tyler. "Security?"

"Yeah," Jeremy answered. "I think they make robots, including some for the army."

R-r-rumble!

The big metal door rolled upward.

A robot appeared in the opening.

It was over ten feet tall. Sharp-looking saw blades rotated on its shoulders. It raised a mechanical arm with a strange glowing weapon and pointed it at Tyler.

Hummmmmmm. Bzzzzzzzz.

Tyler's head began to throb. His vision started getting blurry. It was getting hard to think.

Boom! Crackle!

A missile flew from a launcher in the robot's other arm. It hit the doors behind Tyler. Glass shattered, and the impact knocked him to the ground.

The machine stepped forward.

It towered above Tyler. Its blades began to spin.

"Self-destruct countdown activated," it growled.

"The party . . . is . . . about to . . . start."

Aunt Hill

Shane Heinrich didn't feel like doing homework on Wednesday afternoon, so he had plenty of time to watch videos before dinner. He sat down at his desk, opened his laptop, and started searching his favorite channels.

PrankDatLoser, KickMePleez, AtomicTroll. None of them had anything new. Shane kept looking.

SuperVandal, FoeToeBahm5, EncyclopediaCatvidia, N-Sulter, KitchNDsaster. Been there, seen 'em all. He kept scrolling.

DudeDestructo . . . Shane had already watched that

guy drop hundreds of appliances out windows. He seriously needed to find new content.

Shane was starting to get frustrated. Then he spotted a new name on the *Hot Top Twenty* list: Boxabytes77.

The profile pic was an eyeball . . . and Boxabytes77 had more than *sixty million* followers!

Shane went right to the playlist:

Boxabytes? The video titles seemed weird, too, but Shane didn't care. He wanted new stuff. He clicked on *Cookies with Miss Mantis*.

The video loaded for a few seconds, then started. A little girl, maybe six years old, sat at a table covered with a red checkered tablecloth. Her hair was separated into two neat French braids, and she was wearing a puffy-sleeved dress. In one hand, she clutched an old-fashioned doll and held it above a toy table with two toy chairs and tiny cups and plates.

"Ugh!" said Shane.

This was Boxabytes77? Judging from the name, he had hoped for videos that featured people getting bitten, or punched . . . or maybe even bitten *and* punched. But it didn't look like this girl was going to do any fighting or biting. It was all unboxing videos.

And this . . . was the worst unboxing video Shane had ever seen.

"This is Happy Heidi. Who did she invite to her tea party today?" asked the girl, waving the doll. "Who wants to have fun?"

Boxabytes77 sure didn't look like *she* was having fun. She stared down at the tablecloth without showing any emotion. Slowly, she pressed the doll into one of the toy chairs, then held up a new doll, still in its packaging.

"Oh, look," she said flatly. "Miss Mantis is here."

Shane scratched his head. Thirty million views . . . for this?

The girl unwrapped a doll of a lady in a winter coat. She pressed it into the other toy chair and then pretended to pour tea for both dolls.

Nobody got sprayed in the face with a volcano of diet soda and Mentos. Nobody stepped on a nail and dropped their science fair project.

The girl picked up Happy Heidi and shook the doll at Miss Mantis.

"It's so nice of you to visit," she said, pretending to speak in the doll's voice. "Do you think it will rain this weekend?"

Shane wasn't interested in hearing Miss Mantis's thoughts about the weather. He clicked on the link to *Mr. Froggy LIKES Peppermint*. That video had more than eleven million views.

"Who is having tea with us today?" Boxabytes77 asked with no emotion.

Once again, she held Happy Heidi as she unwrapped a new doll, a fuzzy green frog doll in a tiny top hat. She placed it in the chair across from Happy Heidi. Then she pretended to serve tea.

"I like peppermint," croaked the girl in a froglike voice.

She picked up Happy Heidi and shook her at Mr. Froggy.

"Would you like some . . . *punch?*" she asked.

Shane smiled. Maybe now it was going to get good. He used that joke on his friends all the time. He'd asked someone if they wanted punch . . . and then he'd punch them in the face.

"No thank you," the girl said in Mr. Froggy's voice. "But let me tell you about flowers I saw on the way to this party. There were petunias . . . daffodils . . . daisies . . ."

"Yuck," said Shane.

He didn't want flowers. He wanted a fight.

"Roses . . . buttercups . . . ," the girl continued.

Shane glanced at the stats below the video. This *tea party* was an hour and a half long. If he was going to spend that much time watching something, it better feature someone falling out of a tree, or getting scratched

by angry kittens, or cutting their head on the blades of a rotating ceiling fan.

"Carnations . . . begonias . . . tulips . . ."

Mr. Froggy was *still* talking about flowers.

Shane looked at the comments underneath *Mr. Froggy LIKES Peppermint*.

" 'Genius entertainment value,' " he read.

There were thousands of comments. Every one of them glowed with praise.

" 'It's the greatest show that has ever been on a screen,' " said Shane, reading another.

This didn't make sense at all. He had watched more than ten thousand hours of videos. This was definitely not the greatest show that has ever been on a screen. If anything, this was in the running for dumbest and most boring video. Of all time.

But . . . *Mr. Froggy LIKES Peppermint* had more than *eleven million* views. How could that be?

"Shane!"

Through the bedroom door, he heard his mother calling from downstairs. She could wait. This was a mystery Shane needed to solve. He scrolled down to more comments.

"'Amazing and captivating,'" Shane read, scratching his head.

Moving on, he clicked on *Biscuits OMG! with Aunt Hillary.* According to the playlist, it had almost forty million views. Maybe he'd see something to help him understand what this was all about.

Nope.

Boxabytes77 unwrapped another boring old doll. She placed "Aunt Hill" at the table.

"Did you know . . . ," the girl said in a phony fake British accent, "where I come from, we say 'biscuits' when we mean 'cookies'?"

Shane didn't know this . . . and he really didn't care.

"Why, Aunt Hill," said the girl, switching to Happy Heidi. "That is so interesting. I would love to hear more while we enjoy these cookies—I mean, biscuits."

"Shane!" his mother called from downstairs again.

Were they really going to talk about cookies, or biscuits, or whatever, for a full hour and forty-seven minutes? He skipped ahead to the end of *Biscuits OMG! with Aunt Hillary* so the video only had two minutes left.

"Shane!" called his mother. "We ordered pizza!"

"I can hear you!" Shane shouted, rising from his chair.

He'd seen enough of these stupid videos. Somehow, they had millions and millions of fans. But Aunt Hill was just as dumb as Mr. Froggy or Miss Mantis. Possibly dumber.

Swish. Clatter!

Shane turned back to his computer. On-screen, Boxabytes77 swept her arm across the table. Aunt Hill and all of the teacups and the biscuits went flying.

Music began to play. It sounded like an old-fashioned piano. Several of the notes were out of tune.

Swish. Clatter!

She brushed away the rest of the chairs and the toy table.

"Huh?" muttered Shane.

The girl held Happy Heidi up to the camera . . . and its porcelain face fell off.

Happy Heidi was hiding something horrible! A twitching insect face filled the screen. Long, segmented antennae wiggled over its head. It looked like a giant ant, or maybe a termite.

"I am Boxabug," it said. "My guest had to leave." Now I can spend some special time . . . with . . . *you*."

The strange face spoke directly to the camera. It wasn't the girl talking. The sound definitely came from the insect. The voice was a low, chittering rasp.

Shane glanced around the room. Was this a prank?

"Look at me," the insect commanded. "Sit . . . down!"

Shane sat back down at his desk. It happened automatically. He faced the laptop with eyes wide open.

"This is the greatest show that has ever been on any screen," growled the insect, snapping its mandibles between words. "It has genius . . . entertainment . . . value."

Shane stared into the dark compound eyes. He tried to turn his head away, but it felt like someone was holding him in place, pointing him at the screen. Sweat beaded on the back of his neck.

Red hairs bristled and twitched around the creature's head as it spoke. Shane felt a wave of prickly jolts running up and down his spine.

"You will . . . subscribe to me . . . and you will watch all of my videos," said the insect. "You will show my videos to your family and friends . . . and they will show them to all of their friends. Everyone must know that my show is amazing and captivating."

Shane leaned in closer so the screen was just a few

inches from his face. His eyes were getting dry. They burned, but he didn't blink.

"You will rewatch all of my videos every week," said the insect. "Then, when my tea party has more than one hundred million . . . guests . . . I will give the signal. You will all rise up and follow my instructions, and we will begin to build. And eat. And build."

"Shane!" his mother called, much louder than before. "We started dinner! Your pizza's getting cold!"

The video ended. Shane leaned back and looked away from the computer.

"Shane!" his mother's voice boomed. "Can you hear?"

He stood up. He switched off the laptop.

"Yes, Mom!" he shouted, opening his bedroom door. "I hear you!"

Shane glanced at the blank screen. Then he walked down the stairs, entered the dining room, and sat down at the table between his parents. He lifted the lid of the pizza box in the center of the table.

Suddenly, the cheese made him feel queasy. He looked away, letting the box lid flop closed.

"Were you playing a game up there?" asked his dad.

"Nah," said Shane. "I was just watching videos and stuff."

He began to stare at the arm of his chair. His mouth watered.

"Haven't you already seen every mean, rotten video there is?" asked his sister from across the table.

He didn't look at her. He kept staring at his chair.

"I was watching something amazing and captivating," he said, pulling out his phone.

Without looking up, he tapped at the screen. The sound of an old-fashioned piano began to play.

"Watch this," said Shane.

He held out his phone so everyone at the table could see.

Crack!

While his family stared at the screen, Shane used his free hand to snap the arm from his chair. He began gnawing at the wood.

"See?" Shane asked through a mouthful of sawdust. "It has genius . . . entertainment . . . value."

Bobble

Krista McClurken was the biggest sports fan in the world. At least, that's what she told everyone. She was actually the biggest *sports collectible* fan in the world. She had thousands of cards, posters, bottle caps, and ticket stubs for every sports team in Chicago.

Some of her collection was valuable. Some of it was really valuable. And some of it was priceless.

Krista had the only known poster signed by the moms of every player on the 1986 Superbowl Champion Bears team. She owned a complete set of basketball shoes,

socks, shorts, and underwear all signed by Michael Jordan. Those were awesome, but where she really had everyone beat was her treasure trove of Chicago Cubs *everything*.

Krista's Cubs collection included caps, rookie cards, cereal boxes, and every kind of pin, sticker, and snow globe. Above her bedroom door hung a baseball bat autographed by the entire 2016 World Series–winning team. She kept a scale model of Wrigley Field on her dresser.

Her most prized possession, however, was a collection of thirty-nine super-rare Cubs bobbleheads lining the long shelf on her bedroom wall. Sometimes she placed them in chronological order. Other times, she arranged them by how much money they were worth. They were worth a lot! Every night, when Krista entered her room, she stomped on the floor. It made her smile to see all the little heads jiggle at the same time.

Krista was proud of her collection. She had built it all by herself, through shrewd buying, selling, and trading.

And cheating.

Krista had major league talent for bargaining, and just as much talent for deceiving and leaving out facts here and there. She loved convincing people to sell valuable items to her for pennies. Once, she forged a Babe Ruth signature on a baseball and traded it for a *real* signed Ernie Banks first baseman's glove.

Krista's parents used to encourage her hobby. They were proud when the most popular sports-trading website in the US, *Collectiblast*, featured her on their home page. They were happy to take her to conventions and swap meets and fan conferences. And it was easy to figure out what to get for her birthday present.

Then, little by little, the house filled with stuff. T-shirts and big foam "We're #1" fingers packed the closets. Flags, programs, and posters piled up under every chair and coffee table. It became impossible for her parents to find a birthday present for Krista.

"I already have one of those," she would say, no matter what. "Besides, those aren't worth more than two lousy dollars."

More worrisome for her parents, Krista's grades began to drop.

"Kiddo," said her father as she passed through the living room, "you need to start paying as much attention to school as you do to sports."

Krista rolled her eyes. When her dad used the word *kiddo*, she knew he was trying to be nice, but it always meant that bad news was coming.

Her mother waved a blue envelope. Blue envelopes meant that the school was worried and another warn-the-parents-about-bad-grades letter had come.

"We've decided not to take you to Swap Mania next week," said her father. "Not unless you can raise your math grade."

"Swap Mania?" cried Krista. "That's the biggest trading event of the year. They're expecting me. I have to show up."

"Only if you can improve your grades," said her mother. Mrs. McClurken unfolded the letter and scanned it. "From a C-minus," she read, "to at least a B."

Krista stomped around the house, shouting that her parents didn't understand anything about sports, or hobbies, or kids. She raged and ranted about promises, dealmaking, and what she would do differently as a parent. Then, to top it off, she knocked over a display of hockey-star soda cans.

After she cooled down an hour later, she came back and calmly agreed to attend math do-over day at school that Saturday. Two hours of study time, and then a makeup test.

Krista didn't think she'd need more than a few hours to catch up on math, and then she'd do just fine on the test.

Grade saved. Problem solved. Swap Mania, here we come.

"I'll see you this afternoon!" Krista shouted on Saturday morning as she skipped down the stairs. "I'm off to win at math!"

She hopped over a pile of mini football helmets, turned left at a case of hockey player mugs, and opened the front door . . . where a package rested on the porch.

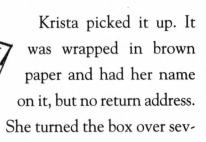

Krista picked it up. It was wrapped in brown paper and had her name on it, but no return address. She turned the box over several times and inspected it. Nothing. No information about who sent it.

Anyone else might have considered an unmarked box strange, but packages with Krista's name on them showed up at the house all the time. She was always working on a trade, or a scam or swindle. A few weeks ago, she'd written a heartwarming letter to the Baseball Hall of Fame. She claimed her grandfather had lent a pair of shoes to Jackie Robinson to wear in the 1955 World Series, and that his dying wish was to get them back so his "precious baby princess Kristalina" could wear the shoes while she cared for endangered animals in the Amazon rain forest. It was a completely made-up story, but this mysterious package was about the size of a shoebox. Maybe her letter had worked.

She carried the box inside the house, set it on the kitchen counter, and carefully cut away the tape with a knife.

She opened the box.

A face smiled up at her.

It was a bobblehead.

Krista lifted up the doll and searched inside the box for a note or a letter to explain who had sent the package. Nothing.

She tried to remember all the other rip-offs, or tricks, or dishonest schemes that she had worked on recently, but she couldn't think of one that involved a bobblehead.

Where did this package come from?

She looked at the figurine.

It had a little black cap and the kind of uniform the Cubs had worn in the early twentieth century, about a hundred years ago. Krista squinted at the base of the statue:

The oldest item in Krista's collection was a baseball signed by Mordecai "Three Finger" Brown. He pitched for the Cubs in 1916. The ball was worth more than ten thousand dollars, and this bobblehead was even older. She had never even heard of a Cub named Knob. Who knew how much it was worth? And who had sent it to her?

It didn't matter. It was an amazing collectible.

She carried the statue up to her room, tiptoeing so her parents wouldn't hear that she was still home. She would just take a quick look at Knob, then hurry straight to her math test.

She closed her bedroom door, put the bobblehead on her desk, and reached for her copy of *Bixby's Book of Baseball Bargains*.

There was not a single mention of any player with the name Knob.

She reached for *Henderson's Home Run Hobby Handbook*. She kept the old heavy encyclopedia by her bed. Sometimes she'd read it to help her fall asleep.

"Knob," she repeated as she opened the book and began flipping back and forth.

Nothing. No mention of a Cub named Knob.

Who was he? And how much was the bobblehead worth?

She kept searching but still didn't find anything.

Then she remembered do-over day and looked at the clock.

Time had flown by while she'd been reading. It was nine-thirty! Krista had already missed most of her study time, and the test would start at ten.

She grabbed her 2016 Cubs commemorative lunch box, put Knob inside, and zipped it shut. Then she raced downstairs and out the door.

Still carrying her lunch box, she got to the school library at nine-fifty-five.

"Just in time," said the teacher, dropping a number-two pencil and a quiz packet onto the desk as Krista took her seat.

She took a deep breath and picked up the pencil, preparing for the worst.

It *was* the worst!

Eleven pages of tricky math problems, plus a multiple-choice section. Even if Krista had made it back in time for several hours of review, she doubted she'd be able to pass this test. She filled in a circle to answer the first question. After that, she was stuck. She had no idea how to answer the second question. She flipped ahead. Nope. She couldn't answer that one either.

She flipped through the packet, hoping to find a few easy questions. Then she groaned softly and gave up. She raised her hand.

"Can I leave now?" she asked the teacher. "I answered all the questions I can."

"Sorry," he replied. "Once the test starts, you have to stay until every student is finished."

Krista let out a second, longer frustrated groan. What an awful day. When she got home, her parents would find out about this test, and then it would be over. No Swap Mania!

Her foot bumped her lunch box under the desk. She had forgotten about the statue. She reached down, unzipped the insulated lunch box, and took out the bobblehead. She placed it on the desk a little harder than she'd intended. It clattered as it hit the tabletop and its head wobbled.

"Knob," Krista said softly, reading the molded letters on the base of the statue. "How come I've never heard of you before?"

As she watched the smiling ball player's head rocking back and forth, she noticed a large red scratch along its forehead.

"Just my luck," muttered Krista.

A damaged collectible was worth a lot less than one in mint condition.

She sighed and touched the mark with her finger. It wasn't a scratch after all. It was a smooth indentation, painted bright red. Whoever made this bobblehead had added a big red scar on purpose. Very odd. She shook the statue gently, making it wobble again.

The head came to a stop at an angle. The little ballplayer seemed to be looking down at her answer sheet.

"At least I got one right," said Krista.

Then she took a closer look at the bobblehead's eyes. They seemed to be staring at the last circle in the row, not the one that she had filled in.

"You think so?" she whispered.

Krista glanced at the question again, and—she had made a mistake. The answer *was* the last choice.

"Great," said Krista. "Even a bobblehead knows more than I do."

She bit her lip and looked at the figurine again.

She tapped its head and watched it wobble. When it came to a stop, it was staring at a circle in the second row on the answer sheet.

"Really?" she asked.

"No talking!" the teacher called from across the cafeteria.

Krista read the sec-
ond question again.

Knob was
right!

She
filled in
the circle
and turned the
page.

For the next
hour, Krista tapped

the bobblehead over and over, filling in circles where the strange eyes pointed whenever they came to a stop.

"How did it go?" Krista's dad asked when she walked in the front door.

Mr. and Mrs. McClurken sat on the sofa, waiting for the results of math makeup day.

"I . . . got . . . ," said Krista, making them wait for it, ". . . an A-plus!"

She held up the test papers and threw them into the air, letting them flutter around her parents' feet. She stood beaming as they picked them up.

"This is wonderful," said her mother, reading the answer sheet. "A perfect score."

"I knew you could do it if you applied yourself," said her father.

"Sure, sure," Krista called over her shoulder as she headed up to her room. "Don't forget to buy me that ticket to Swap Mania."

At the top of the stairs, she unzipped the Cubs lunch box and took out her new limited-edition collectible. She slid the box into a rack reserved for National League lunch boxes and thermoses.

She stepped into her room, stomped, and watched her bobbleheads shake. Then she crossed to her desk and sat down.

"1903," she read from the base of the statue.

Krista set Knob on her desk, opened her laptop, and continued her search for information about this very old, very mysterious Cub.

Nothing.

She scanned websites and online databases.

No mention of any Chicago baseball player by that name, first or last.

Determined, she pored over team photos for any sign of him.

Still nothing. Very strange.

Krista closed her laptop and opened her desk drawer. She took out *Crandall's Complete Card Compendium* and flipped to the twentieth-century section. She scanned every team roster from 1901 to 1950.

Knob wasn't there.

"Who *are* you?" she said to the bobblehead.

Knob grinned silently. His oval eyes stared at her.

Krista tapped the little statue's head and watched it wobble. When it came to a stop, it wasn't pointing at her anymore. Knob's head had tilted back at an angle. Krista followed his gaze up to the long shelf above her bed, lined with her prized bobbleheads.

"I get it," said Krista. "You want to hang out with some friends."

She picked up Knob and carried him to the shelf. Standing on the foot of her bed, she placed him at the far right, where there was room for one last statue. When she stepped back down, she noticed all the other heads were jiggling. Had she bumped the shelf?

Krista watched her thirty-nine rare Cubs shake while Knob stood there, not moving. It was as if all the other dolls were nervous to be around him. Weird.

"Okay. No sense in upsetting anyone," she said.

Krista reached for the glass dome resting on the night-stand. It contained her autographed Ernie Banks glove. She pushed it to one side to clear a space. Then she took Knob down from the shelf and set him next to her bed.

"Much better," she said.

Krista went to brush her teeth and then she changed into her Chicago Cubs pajamas and got into bed.

She had trouble falling asleep. Every time Krista closed her eyes, she pictured Knob, grinning and wobbling. There was something odd about the way the little statue had smiled as it looked at her during the math test. And how it stared at her from her bedside table. It took Krista a long time to fall asleep.

In her dreams, Krista pictured a baseball game in which a real player who looked like Knob was at bat. But the player wasn't swinging at a ball. Instead, he was stumbling around home plate. He had a big gash on his forehead, and blood streamed down his face. He wobbled, stumbled, and . . .

Krista opened her eyes and looked over at her nightstand. The glow from her baseball-shaped night-light lit Knob's head from behind. Light blazed from his eyes as he grinned at her.

She felt a shudder and looked away. There was definitely something creepy about the little statue, with its wide smile and bright red scar.

Krista got out of bed, picked up Knob, and carried him across the room.

"Perfect," she said, setting him on a table made from three baseball bats held together on top by a home plate. "That's a fine stand for a super-rare, limited-edition collectible."

She tapped Knob's forehead, right on the red scar.

It didn't move. He stared at her.

"Have it your way," she said. "Don't bobble."

She shrugged and climbed back into bed.

Much better. She went back to sleep.

A deep sleep.

Everything was just fine.

"Take me out to the ball game!"

Krista opened her eyes.

It was early Sunday morning. She was pretty sure she hadn't set her MLB alarm clock the night before.

"Take me out to the crowd!"

She sat up. The clock flashed 6:00 a.m. in bright figures.

"Take me out to the ball game!"

"Okay, okay," she said, slapping the Snooze button.
Krista froze.

A few inches from her fingertips, beside her clock, Knob stood smiling on the nightstand. Had she carried him there in the night? She clearly remembered placing him across the room on her home plate table. Shaken, she got out of bed and dressed quickly.

As Krista brushed her hair, she caught a glimpse of Knob in the mirror on her dresser. The little statue's head pointed upward, facing the shelf with her prized bobbleheads.

She walked over and used her fingers to twist his head forward. Then she let go carefully, making sure not to start the wobbling.

She thought about the wobbling, staggering player in her dream.

"1903." She read the molded numbers on his base. "What happened that year?"

Krista raised her eyebrows.

"That *exciting year in baseball*," she said knowingly.

Then she turned and headed out of her room.

As Krista's collection grew and grew, the McClurken house ran out of wall space for her shelves, cabinets, and display cases. Krista had started storing her less precious keepsakes in the basement, including most of her sports-related books.

She went to the kitchen and opened the door that led to the basement. There, she began to search among the boxes of worn reference books. Most of them had torn covers or cracked spines. None were in good condition. None were valuable. There wasn't a big market for encyclopedias or yearbooks these days, now that you could look anything up on the internet.

Well, *almost* anything. She couldn't find Knob.

"Record books, almanacs, histories," Krista said, reading labels on boxes stacked five high. "Yearbooks."

She took down the box of yearbooks, set it on the

floor, and began to flip through musty albums. She pulled out a heavy volume:

THIS EXCITING YEAR IN BASEBALL
1903 Edition

The book had a cracked leather cover. It smelled like sweaty shoes. Krista opened it carefully so the whole thing wouldn't fall apart. She flipped through dusty, yellowed pages until she found a chapter about baseball in Chicago:

"Rodolphus Knob?" Krista asked breathlessly.

CHICAGO'S "CUBS"
The Young Stars Had a Humdinger of a Season

Doc Casey	Bill Hanlon	George Moriarity
Frank Chance	Alex Hardy	Jimmy Slagle
Jim Cook	Johnny Kling	Jack Taylor
Clarence Currie	Bobby Lowe	Joe Tinker
Jack Doscher	Carl Lundgren	Jake Weimer
Peaches Graham	Jack McCarthy	Bob Wicker
Rodolphus Knob	Jerry Mclean	Otto Williams

She flipped through the chapter, scanning all the player summaries. Each Cub had several pages describing their personal histories and highlights for the year. But there was one entry that filled less than half a page.

RODOLPHUS "BOB" KNOB

When rookie Bob Knob took the field in his first game, his wide smile was an instant hit with the fans. Unfortunately, it was not the only memorable hit that hot summer day.

In the first inning, "Big Ed" Delahanty of the Washington Senators hit a line drive that struck Knob on the forehead. The crowd gasped in horror as they watched the poor man's head wobble from side to side like a bushel of apples on a donkey's back. After sixty long, frightful seconds, Knob collapsed and was carried from the stadium on a stretcher.

Two days later, a tourist found Delahanty dead at the bottom of Niagara Falls. Knob disappeared without a trace, so police were never able to question him.

Major League officials are debating what to do with Knob's history, as this sordid tale may tarnish the sport's sterling reputation.

Krista closed the cover. The officials must have decided not to include this story in any record books. That explained why she had never heard of a Cub named Knob.

She thought about the red scar on the bobblehead's

temple, and the strange expression on its face. She pictured the real-life Knob, with his head wobbling gruesomely before collapsing on the field.

Footsteps creaked the floorboards above her. Her parents must be in the kitchen. She replaced the yearbook and slid the box back onto the stack.

"Rodolphus Knob," she whispered as she headed up the stairs.

"There she is," said her mother as soon as Krista entered the kitchen.

"We've been waiting for you, kiddo," said her father.

He held up a plastic card on a lanyard:

"A gold pass!" said Krista.

"You did such a great job yesterday," said her mother. "We got you a special present."

Krista couldn't believe it. Swap Mania gold passes were expensive, and hard to find, too. If you had one, you could use the special red-carpet entrance, attend the opening-night gala, and sell one item at the VIP auction.

"You really did it," said her father. "You showed us you could work as hard at studying as you do at collecting."

"Whatever," said Krista, snatching the lanyard.

She looped it around her neck. Then she held up the laminated card and shook it at both of them.

"You're driving me to Swap Mania at five a.m. on Saturday," she told them. "I don't want to miss any of the events. And I know exactly what I'm going to sell at the VIP auction, too. I've got this *creepy* doll from 1903, and—"

Krista stopped mid-sentence. Through the space between her parents, she spotted Knob perched on the kitchen counter, smiling and nodding.

"How did *that* get down here?" she asked.

"What exactly?" asked her mother, turning to look. "The New York Knicks knife sharpener? The Dallas Cowboys cookie jar?"

"I think she means that Detroit Red Wings spice rack," said her father, pointing above the sink. "Or maybe the Tiger Woods can opener."

Krista wasn't sure if her parents were being sarcastic, or maybe the kitchen was so full of sports collectibles, they didn't notice something new and strange—and wobbling and grinning.

"Never mind," said Krista, pushing past them.

She grabbed Knob by his head.

"Stay here," she told them, heading out of the kitchen. "I'll be right back, and we'll make plans for Swap Mania."

Krista marched up to her bedroom, swinging Knob by the head. She wondered how the little statue had wound up on the counter. She was positive she hadn't put it there. And had Knob been listening when she said she was going to sell him at the VIP auction? Could a bobble-head hear things? Did he care? It didn't matter. She had had enough of the odd doll with the strange smile and the big scar. She was going to sell him as soon as she could.

She hopped onto her bed and set Knob down at the end of her special shelf.

"Enjoy it here while you can," she said as she stepped back onto the floor.

She stomped.

All the Cubs jiggled, except for Knob. His head stayed still, pointing to his right as if he were watching all the others.

"Wobble," said Krista.

She stomped her foot again, much harder.

All the bobbleheads shook, including Knob, but his head came to rest quickly. He stared forward and down, looking directly at Krista.

"I said wobble!" she barked at him, raising her foot.

Before she could stomp again, her parents called from the kitchen.

"Krista!" her mother shouted. "Are you coming back? We're planning snacks for the trip Saturday."

"I'll deal with you later," she hissed at Knob, and left the room.

On her way downstairs, she bumped a shelf with her elbow. A case with a cereal box featuring Scottie Pippen of the Chicago Bulls tumbled down the steps ahead of her. It smacked into a commemorative 1998 Chicago Bears toaster. She knelt at the bottom and picked up the box. It was fine. Then she inspected the toaster. A big scratch ran across the team logo.

The toaster was no longer in mint condition. It had just lost a ton of value, and it was Knob's fault!

No. That was ridiculous.

Krista took a deep breath. She was letting a little statue upset her. *She* was the one who had bumped the cereal box. Everything was fine.

The more she thought about it, the sillier everything seemed. That story about Knob getting hit by a line drive was probably something somebody made up to sell yearbooks. Was there even a baseball player named "Big Ed" Delahanty?

And that math test. It was a lucky coincidence that she picked all the correct answers, that's all.

She took another deep breath and felt better.

"Kiddo!" her father called. "Are you on your way?"

Krista knew what would make her feel a whole lot better: bargaining.

"I'm walking the red carpet next Saturday," she told her parents as she entered the kitchen. "I'll need a new pair of shoes."

"New shoes?" her mother asked. "For a swap meet?"

"I can't afford to look cheap," Krista replied.

"But, kiddo," said her father. "We already spent two hundred dollars on the gold pass."

"Don't you know how hard I worked on that math test?" she barked at him. "I got every question right."

She paced around her parents, rubbing her hands together.

"Tell you what," said Krista. "If you don't buy new shoes, you'll save a lot of money. Maybe a hundred bucks."

"A hundred?" asked her mother.

"Shoes are expensive," Krista answered. "Let's split the difference, and you can just give me sixty dollars to spend on collectibles while I'm at Swap Mania."

"Sixty?" asked her father.

"Per shoe," she replied. "And if I were you, I'd agree to it right away. Before the price goes up."

After an hour and a half of negotiating, she convinced her parents to get up at three a.m. on Saturday and wash their car so it would be sparkling clean for the ride to Swap Mania. They also agreed to pay for a lifetime subscription to *Collectiblast* and to buy her a set of luggage for all the things she was going to buy that day.

Krista marched up to her room feeling *much* better. She pushed open her door and stomped triumphantly.

She gasped. No statues wobbled at her from the shelf. Her precious collection of Cub bobbleheads was destroyed!

Ron Santo was missing both arms. Sammy Sosa had a dozen holes in his head. Billy Williams lay on his back with his legs snapped off at the knees. Krista's super-rare Hank Sauer figurine had been completely shredded. One small section of his face

resting on top of a mound of slivered plastic was the only recognizable piece.

Arms, legs, ears, noses, and eyeballs were everywhere. Only one bobblehead wasn't wrecked.

Knob stood on the shelf, smiling and nodding.

Krista leapt onto her bed and snatched the little statue.

"Did you do this?" she asked angrily.

Nothing. Knob stared and smiled.

Krista tapped him on the head, right on his scar.

"I said, *Did you do this?*" she asked again.

Knob stared.

She poked him on the bright red scar a dozen times, forcing his little head backward with each tap.

"Answer me!"

Click.

Knob's mouth sprang open, revealing rows of gleaming white teeth. *Razor-sharp* gleaming white teeth. His mouth looked like the inside of a tiny, wobbling shark!

Clack!

His mouth snapped shut on Krista's finger.

"Yow!" she shouted, and tumbled backward onto her bed.

Knob's mouth was still clamped tightly around her index finger. The teeth dug into her like little needles. She shook her hand to get it loose, but his jaws held on tight. It stung like crazy!

Desperately, Krista swung her hand and slammed him into the framed poster signed by the moms of the 1986 Bears. The glass shattered and Knob let go. She rolled off the bed and onto the floor.

Lying facedown on her Chicago sports logo rug, she pulled up her hand and inspected her finger. Tiny drops of blood circled her finger as it throbbed with pain.

Krista glanced around the room.

She didn't see Knob anywhere.

She listened.

She didn't hear anything.

Slowly, Krista began to crawl toward her bedroom door. She kept low to the floor.

Still no sign of Knob.

Krista held her breath and inched forward as quietly as possible.

She made it to the door. She reached for the doorknob.

Scra-a-a-ape!

Krista looked up. Her model Wrigley Field was sliding over the edge of her dresser.

Crash!

The heavy plaster model struck her head and shattered into a thousand pieces.

Krista sat there, stunned and dizzy from the blow. She touched her face and it felt moist. She stood up slowly and reached for the mirror on top of her dresser.

A slimy gash ran down her forehead. Blood trickled into her eyes. As she stared at her face in the mirror, she spotted her home plate table.

Across the room, Knob perched on the stand, bobbling and staring at her with his awful grin.

She squinted into the mirror at the letters beneath his feet.

"Bonk," said Krista, reading the backward letters in the mirror.

The whole room began to spin.

Her head wobbled from side to side.

After sixty long, frightful seconds, she collapsed to the floor.

Krista sat on the edge of her bed.

She heard footsteps in the hall and her door swung open.

"What's going on?" her father asked.

She tried to speak, but her mouth wouldn't move.

Her mother gasped. "Your forehead!"

Krista tried to reply, but her mouth still wouldn't move. Her lips ached. It felt like they stretched into a wide grin.

"Can you understand anything I'm saying?" asked her father.

As she strained to move her head, the world around her seemed to jiggle and shake.

"Kiddo?"

She stared at her father with wide oval eyes.

Her head jiggled.

Up and down.

Side to side.

The Final Page

Ashwin O'Connor stole a book from the game store.

He didn't need to steal it. He had plenty of money. He just didn't feel like paying.

Besides, the guy behind the counter didn't notice him. He just stared at his phone as if there wasn't anyone else in the store. Serves him right.

Ashwin stuffed the paperback into his pocket, walked out, and didn't peek until he got home.

"Meh," he grunted. "It's a puzzle book."

Ashwin flipped to the first page, put a finger on the word *start*, and traced a path, reading letters as he went.

"S . . . T . . . O . . ."

"Stop reading?" Ashwin asked. "Close the book right now?"

Everyone was *always* telling him things *not* to do. And how he shouldn't stick out his foot and trip kids in the hallway. And not to steal things.

In science class, the teacher nagged Ashwin to stop mixing explosive chemicals. At soccer practice, the coach told him he couldn't climb high tension electrical poles. On a field trip, the principal said he shouldn't sneak into the Komodo dragon habitat. Shouldn't . . . couldn't . . . stop . . . don't . . . blah, blah, blah! Ashwin didn't feel like following any more rules or instructions, especially not from a dumb book he didn't even pay for.

He turned to a page in the middle.

The picture didn't make sense. It didn't look like anything . . . until he held the book up and let light shine
through the paper.

"It's too late?" Ashwin asked.

He flipped to the end of the book.

The final page was blurry.

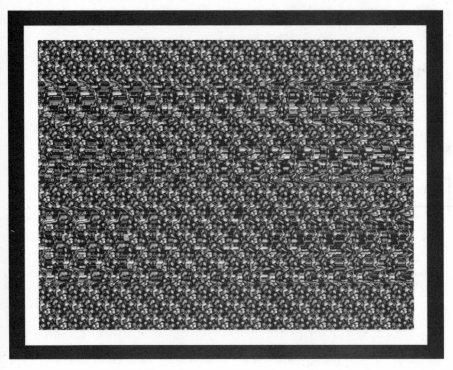

He focused his eyes as if he was looking past the picture into the distance.

Very slowly, he moved the page away from him.

He kept staring. He relaxed.

Three words appeared.

After Words

Sometimes, it's important to write down everything that you see and hear. Other times, it's more important to drop your pen or toss your computer on the floor and get away as soon as possible.

That's what I've decided to do.

I spent a lot of time discovering, and thinking, and tap-tap-tapping words with one finger. It took me a full year to type all these stories.

At least, I think it was a year. I used to own a kitty-cat clock, but its shifting eyes and swinging tail really scared me. I threw it away. Then I got rid of all my calendars. I was always checking to see if anyone secretly circled any of the dates to warn me about awful things that will happen in the future. It was exhausting. But now I'm never really sure what time or day it is.

But there are some things I definitely know for sure.

ONE: If someone warns you not to do something or else an unspeakable horror will appear and you will be eliminated, take them seriously.

TWO: Think twice about bringing something incredibly creepy into your house, and setting it by your nightstand, and then going to sleep with it a few feet from your face.

THREE: Don't get too close to birds.

You've been warned and, when you're done with all this counting . . .

SCREAM!

R.U. GINNS

About the Author

R. U. GINNS lives in a building close to a bridge, just outside a major American city. He collects books, graphic novels, take-out menus, and old catalogs and spends countless hours sifting through them, trying to decide which things are made up and which are real. He knows that the more horrible and terrifying a story is, the greater the chance that it is one hundred percent true.

You can learn more about him at 123SCREAM.com, but that's probably not a good idea. Actually, don't look at that website at all . . . ever!

About the Illustrator

JAVIER ESPILA is a Spanish illustrator who has been devouring cartoons ever since he was old enough to sit upright in front of the TV. This had the unfortunate consequence of causing serious inflammation of the brain, rendering him unsuitable for any job that required him to lift anything heavier than a pencil. In recent years, his condition has deteriorated, and he is now forced to write absurd and fantastic stories to alleviate the constant pressure on his skull.

He lives with his wife and his two daughters, who help him by alternating cartoons with video games.